A HOLE IN ONE

A GLASS DOLPHIN MYSTERY

JUDY PENZ SHELUK

Superior Shores Press

PRAISE FOR THE GLASS DOLPHIN MYSTERIES

The Hanged Man's Noose (#1)

"A thoroughly engaging debut mystery… well-plotted, well-paced and just plain well done!" — *Elizabeth J. Duncan, award-winning author, the PENNY BRANNIGAN and SHAKESPEARE IN THE CATSKILLS mystery series*

"A small town with a dark past, its inhabitants full of secrets, a ruthless developer, and an intrepid reporter with secrets of her own come together to create a can't-put-down-read." — *Vicki Delany, bestselling author of the SHERLOCK HOLMES BOOKSHOP mystery series*

"Compelling characters with hidden connections and a good, old-fashioned amateur sleuth getting in over her head." — *James M. Jackson, author of the SEAMUS MCCREE mystery series*

A Hole in One (#2)

"What fun! A twisty tale chock full of clues and red herrings, antiques and secrets, and relationships that aren't what they seem." — *Jane K. Cleland, award-winning author, JOSIE PRESCOTT ANTIQUES mysteries and MASTERING PLOT TWISTS*

"A bang-up mystery! Two friends, two murders, secret pasts, and a touch of romance. Who could ask for more?" — *Lea Wait, USA TODAY bestselling author, SHADOWS ANTIQUE PRINT and MAINELY NEEDLEPOINT mystery series*

"A well-constructed, well-paced mystery tale grounded in an eclectic cast of characters…a puzzling murder set against a believable portrait of village life…and a fun read that is perfectly paced." *Jim Napier for THE OTTAWA REVIEW OF BOOKS*

PRAISE FOR THE MARKETVILLE MYSTERIES

Skeletons in the Attic (#1)

"A smartly constructed mystery in the good old-fashioned and highly readable sense." — *Jack Batten,* THE TORONTO STAR

"Callie's plight grabs the reader from the get-go and, as the plot twists and twists again, you follow her with heart in mouth. Is there any way for this to end well? Yes, there is, and you won't see it coming!"— *Catriona McPherson, award-winning author of* THE REEK OF RED HERRINGS

Past & Present (#2)

"A tense, emotionally gripping, multifaceted mystery that serves both as a perfect continuation of Callie's life story and as a fine stand-alone read for newcomers." — *MIDWEST BOOK REVIEW*

"Sheluk nails it with this intriguing mystery that stitches together an investigation into the past with people's lives in the present— including that of protagonist Callie Barnstable. Treat yourself to a new present-day read—you won't be disappointed." — *Edith Maxwell, author of the Agatha-nominated* QUAKER MIDWIFE *mystery series*

A Fool's Journey (#3)

"A compelling page-turning mystery you won't want to miss." – *Rick Mofina, USA Today bestselling author of* THE LYING HOUSE

"A well-crafted mystery with fabulous characters and a series of twists and turns that keep you hooked until the end." — *Mike Martin, award-winning author of the* SGT. WINDFLOWER *mystery series*

ALSO BY JUDY PENZ SHELUK

NOVELS

Glass Dolphin Mysteries

The Hanged Man's Noose

A Hole in One

Marketville Mysteries

Skeletons in the Attic

Past & Present

A Fool's Journey

SHORT STORY COLLECTIONS

The Best Laid Plans: 21 Stories of Mystery & Suspense (Editor)

Live Free or Tri

Unhappy Endings

SHORT STORIES

Plan D (The Whole She-Bang 2)

Live Free or Die (World Enough and Crime)

Beautiful Killer (Flash and Bang)

Saturdays with Bronwyn (The Whole She-Bang 3)

Goulaigans (The Whole She-Bang 3)

A Hole In One: A Glass Dolphin Mystery #2

Copyright © 2018/2019 Judy Penz Sheluk

Edited by Anita Lock and Ti Locke

Cover art by Hunter Martin

Cover Illustration by S.A. Hadi hasan

Published by Superior Shores Press

ISBN Trade Paperback: 978-1-989495-17-9

ISBN Kindle: 978-1-989495-18-6

First Edition: March 2018

Second Edition: August 2019

For Mike, who keeps on believing

1

ARABELLA CARPENTER RAN her hands over the smooth surface of the shiny new jet ski. It was the hole in one prize at the Second Annual Kids Come First Golf Tournament. The tournament—a charitable initiative supporting program for at-risk youth in the tri-community area of Lount's

Landing, Miakoda Falls, and Lakeside—was being held at the Miakoda Falls Golf and Country Club.

Somehow, Gillian "Gilly" Germaine, the tournament organizer, had convinced her that sponsoring the contest would be good advertising for Arabella's Glass Dolphin antiques shop. Well, "convinced" wasn't entirely accurate. It was her new business partner, Emily Garland, who'd talked her into it, though what jet skis and golf had to do with antiques was beyond Arabella. Nevertheless, their deal was that Emily would be in charge of advertising and promotion, leaving Arabella to concentrate on purchasing and sales. Nixing Emily's first real A&P idea would have been bad form.

Arabella didn't have much choice in the matter. Emily had been adamant. A jet ski, she had explained, would be the kind of prize the well-heeled folks in Lakeside would gravitate toward. The Glass Dolphin sponsoring such a prize would give it the sort of chichi street cred that would make them want to visit the shop. Once they made the twenty-five-minute trek to Lount's Landing, they were bound to buy something. Especially once they saw the quality of the Glass Dolphin's merchandise.

"What if someone actually hit a hole in one and they had to give away the jet ski?" Arabella had asked. Emily had a ready answer. The odds were astronomical. The third hole, a nasty par three, was one hundred and forty yards to carry over a pond, another twenty-five yards to the pin, with a thicket of trees on both sides, and a sand trap that beckoned from behind. Downright nasty it was.

Having played the course on a couple of occasions, Arabella had conceded that number three was challenging. But that didn't make it impossible. Not by a long shot—pun fully intended.

Even better, Emily had countered. "If no one won the jet ski, it would be that day's news, quickly forgotten. But if someone won, imagine the headlines. For sure it would make the local press, but they might even get some coverage in the Toronto papers, not to mention the rampant word-of-mouth machine that ran in the tri-communities."

The sound of a golf cart heading in her direction stopped Arabella's thoughts midstream. She glanced over the green and watched as Emily wound her way along the paved path, a cardboard sign propped up in the basket at the back of the cart. She parked the cart a few feet from where Arabella was standing, hopped off, smoothed out her black golf skort, and positively sprinted over to the jet ski.

As always, Arabella felt a touch of envy at Emily's glossy, dark hair, now neatly tied into a ponytail, her bangs held gently in place by a black and gold Miakoda Falls Golf and Country Club visor. Arabella's own hair was a mass of auburn curls that behaved well enough on a cool, dry, winter's day, but got wilder and woolier as summer's heat and humidity ratcheted up. On a hot, muggy day like today, it was virtually unmanageable. Stick a cap on top of it and she resembled Bozo the clown. Not exactly the look an almost forty-year-old woman was after, but there wasn't much she could do about it. Even if she took the time to flat iron it straight, it would last all of an hour in this heat.

"Gorgeous," Emily was saying, her fingers caressing the jet ski. "Too bad we're ineligible to win.

You know, on the off-chance one of us gets a hole in one."

"I think the odds of that happening are pretty slim." And slim just left town.

"Yeah, you're probably right. Wait 'til you see what I've got." Emily ran back to the golf cart, pulled a gold-lettered placard out of the basket, and inserted it into the rectangular tee sign currently advertising the club's twilight rates, fussing and fidgeting until she got it positioned just right.

"Print It! did a great job, don't you think? Gave us a good deal, too. I think Harvey felt sorry for me, and to be honest, I did milk getting fired from *Inside the Landing* to broker a deal. Plus I let him put his Print It! business logo on the bottom." Emily grinned. "I think that was rather a stroke of genius."

A good cost-saving idea, sure. A stroke of genius? That might be taking things a bit far. "They look great. The sign, the jet ski. Except I'm the one doing the books, and believe me when I tell you, and not for the first time, that the Glass Dolphin is barely breaking even. I'm just not sure we can afford it."

Emily sighed. "First off, it's a bit too late to renege now, the night before the tournament, don't you think? What would that do to our reputation? Second, I've already explained how little money this will actually cost the shop. One good sale should easily cover it. If it makes you feel any better, I'll go over the numbers one last time."

"Humor me."

"Fine. The jet ski is being supplied by Luke's Lakeside Marina. Luke transported it from the marina, at no cost to us, and he'll either take it back to the marina after the tournament, or arrange delivery to the winner, should there be one. He's also springing for half the insurance and fifty percent of the sign, which, as I already told you, is costing us next to nothing. Essentially, we're co-sponsoring the hole with him."

Arabella suspected Emily's relationship with Luke Surmanski ran a lot deeper than co-sponsoring a hole in one contest at a golf tournament, but she let it go. Emily would confide in her when she was ready.

"Explain the insurance again."

This netted another sigh, along with an exaggerated eye roll. "I gave you the policy to read over two weeks ago. Didn't you do that?"

Arabella had meant to, but she'd been busy. Then there'd been that two-day multi-estate auction in Pottageville. She'd won more box lots than expected, and had been sorting through them ever since. It wasn't easy to decide what items to keep for sale in the shop, which to reserve for sale online, and what should be donated to the local ReStore. Before she knew it, the day of the tournament had arrived. She shook her head and did her best to look sufficiently contrite.

The look must have worked, because the exasperation on Emily's face softened ever so slightly. "I'll give you the Reader's Digest version. I went to Stanford McLelland Insurance Brokerage, and you'll be happy to know that I dealt directly with Stanford."

That, at least, made Arabella feel better. Before opening the Glass Dolphin, she'd worked for Stanford doing a variety of claims-related tasks, especially those involving antiques and collectibles. When it came to the insurance business, there wasn't much the man didn't know.

"Stanford found a company that specializes in hole in one insurance. That's all they do, actually."

Incredible. Here they were, trying to diversify to boost sales, and there was a company that did nothing but sell hole in one insurance.

"How does it work?"

"They calculate the number of golfers participating in the tournament, which in this case is nine holes with four golfers per hole for a grand total of thirty-six, minus our foursome, which leaves thirty-two possible winners. Then they calculate the degree of difficulty for the hole along with the value of the prize. The cost for the Glass Dolphin, all in, is two hundred dollars, which we'll split down the middle with Luke's Lakeside Marina."

"It does sound like you have every angle covered."

"That's the spirit. Trust me, nothing will go wrong."

2

THE MORNING of the tournament was picture perfect, a mid-July day which brought cloudless skies, temperatures in the mid-seventies, and the hint of a gentle breeze. Gone was yesterday's intense heat, and while the humidity was forecast to return later in the week, Arabella was grateful for the temporary reprieve. She allowed herself to hope that the change of weather bode well for the success of the tournament and Kids Come First, and in turn, that the jet ski strategy would bring customers into the Glass Dolphin. She hadn't wanted to worry Emily, but the Pottageville purchases had all but obliterated their bank balance. So far, summer sales had been soft. Hot weather sent people to parks, beaches, and ice cream parlors. Shopping for antiques was a long way down on the to-do list.

But today wasn't the time for negative thoughts. Arabella smiled when she thought about the perfume bottle they were donating to the tournament's silent auction. It was part of one of the ten-dollar estate sale box lots she'd bought in Pottageville. In amongst the glass doorknobs, embroidered doilies, and an assortment of what looked like polished rocks, but might have been semi-precious stones or crystals, were a half dozen circa 1890s Herman Tappan clear glass figural perfume bottles. Unmarked, yes, the labels long removed, but definitely signature Tappan if you knew your stuff, which thankfully, the estate sellers had not.

To be fair, the Herman Tappan Perfume Company wasn't a household name in the same way Lalique was. Nonetheless, Tappan had been one of the major American perfume companies during the Victorian era, producing glass novelty perfume bottles shaped like street lamps, ladies' slippers, baseball bats, birds, and more.

Arabella thought donating one of the bottles to a worthy cause would bring more good luck, not to mention the interest it might bring to the Glass Dolphin—so much more on point than a jet ski. She'd studied each of the six bottles in the lot and finally selected a figural bottle of a small girl wrapped in wolf skin fur for the auction.

Levon had been at the same sale, and still couldn't believe he'd missed the perfume bottles. Levon Larroquette was not only her ex-husband, he was also an antiques picker by trade, having taught her most of what she knew. Sure, she'd had to dig a bit under the doorknobs and doilies, but it wasn't like they'd been invisible. When she'd shown him, afterwards, he'd looked slightly annoyed and more than a little embarrassed.

As well he should. Lately he'd been off his game and Arabella blamed Gilly Germaine for his lack of concentration. The self-proclaimed philanthropist had managed to get her French manicured hooks firmly into Levon, and he was beginning to act like a love-struck schoolboy who couldn't concentrate on his studies.

She shook her head, tossed her golf clubs into the back of her aging SUV, and got ready for the drive to Miakoda Falls. It was time to get to the tournament.

Y

ARABELLA TUCKED the Tappan figural perfume bottle inside a small black velvet-lined case—the original box was unfortunately missing. Of course, if it had been intact, the bottle would never have been in a box lot. She placed the case on the white linen tablecloth in the space reserved for the Glass Dolphin. She straightened the bidding sheet for the umpteenth time, and then reread the index card with the details.

> Clear glass figural perfume bottle by the Herman Tappan Perfume Company, New York, NY, c. 1890. Tappan's colognes were aimed at the middle class and the prices affordable. He was quite fond of the glass novelty figural bottle, for which he owned two patents in the 1890s. This figural bottle of a small girl wrapped in a wolf skin fur is valued between $100 to $150.

Emily would tell her she was being obsessive, but when it came to antiques, Arabella couldn't help it. She prided herself on her research and the information she provided. Accuracy mattered every bit as much as authenticity.

It wasn't until Arabella put the index card back in its holder, satisfied it was acceptable, that she noticed Gilly Germaine had put the Glass Dolphin's spot next to Larroquette's Antiques: Pickers & Appraisers. Was this her way of telling Arabella that she was secure in her new relationship with Levon, that she was completely fine with Levon and Arabella remaining friends? Or did she think his donation would outshine hers?

Levon was offering a free estate or household appraisal service: "From basement to attic and every room in between," which in theory sounded incredibly generous, but actually gave him first foot in the door. It didn't guarantee him the commission, but it certainly wouldn't hurt.

Arabella was still debating Gilly's motives when she heard someone slip into the room. Levon sauntered in, a half-smile playing on his lips. It was one of the rare occasions when Levon wasn't dressed head to toe in denim, but Arabella knew the Miakoda Falls Golf and Country Club adhered to a strict dress code typical of the majority of golf courses: collared shirt and long slacks for men, long shorts permissible but in truth often frowned upon, and collared shirts and long slacks and skirts, skorts, or long shorts for women. No matter how relaxed a club's dress code might be, Daisy Dukes and denim were definitely taboo.

Nonetheless, Levon had managed to find a golf shirt in indigo blue to set off his eyes, and the khaki pants he was wearing managed to accentuate every square inch of his physique, which was fit and trim from years of lifting and moving boxes of collectibles and antique furniture. His hair, slightly shaggy and soft brown, with the first hint of gray at the temples, was all but hidden beneath a golf cap that matched the shirt to perfection. Arabella wished she didn't still notice all those details about him—they were divorced, done and done and done again, a reality that by now was more on her than on him—but with Levon it was damn hard not to. Look up "charisma" in the dictionary and you were likely to see a picture of Levon Larroquette. With a half-smile, no less.

"Nice perfume bottle, Bella baby," Levon said. "It should fetch a decent amount. Gilly will be pleased."

Arabella knew Levon was trying to pay her a compliment, but she couldn't help but feel a flash of annoyance. She could care less if Gilly would be pleased. She did care whether the folks at Kids Come First would be pleased. Arabella believed in supporting her community, and from what she'd been reading about the charity, KCF did just that.

She glanced over at the bid sheet for Levon's appraisal service and noted the estimated value at three hundred dollars, double the amount of her perfume bottle. That ticked her off even more. "Your appraisal offer should also do well. Are you sponsoring a hole too?"

A hit below the belt, given the fact that Arabella knew full well he wasn't—she'd studied the sponsor page on the golf course website and tournament brochure with the same intensity she'd given the index card.

Levon, however, didn't rise to the bait. "No. Gilly thought it would be more helpful if I took on the job of Course Marshal."

Of course she would. As marshal, Levon would be expected to report in to Gilly the entire morning.

"I get to zip from hole to hole in a cart, trying to speed up slow play without offending anyone, while making sure nobody's drinking too much once eleven a.m. hits and the cart girl comes around—"

Levon caught her eye and grinned.

They both knew he was referring to Poppy Spencer. The real estate agent was far from a lush, but when she got into the hard lemonade coolers, she had a tendency to forget there was liquor inside them. The Lount's Landing Canada Day celebration on July first had a very inebriated Poppy standing on top of a table at The Hanged Man's Noose and begging for business, her speech slurred and her usually impeccable clothing disheveled. Betsy Ehrlich, the pub's owner, had managed to talk Poppy off the table without incident, and Emily had driven her home, but no one wanted a repeat performance.

"Sounds like you'll be kept busy," Arabella said, trying to block out the thought of Levon at Gilly's beck and call.

"I've got it covered. It's only nine holes, and it's a best ball scramble. That should keep the pace under two and a half hours, even with all the duffers that are bound to be out there playing for a good cause. Everyone should be back in the clubhouse by twelve-thirty at the latest. That leaves plenty of time for folks to view the silent auction items and bid on them before lunch at one fifteen. Gilly has everything arranged, doesn't leave anything to chance. Well, except for the weather, and even that is cooperating."

Levon smiled, the full-on one he tended to keep in reserve, and Arabella felt something tug inside of her. She had heard quite enough about Gilly Germaine and how amazing she was. It wasn't as if she was jealous, exactly, more like she felt Levon slipping away from her little by little. They might not be married any longer, but she never stopping thinking of him as a friend, someone who knew her and loved her, blemishes and all. Since Gilly had arrived on the scene, Levon had become more and more distant. This past month he'd been all but absent. Today was the first time they'd spoken in two weeks.

It didn't help that she'd recently split up with Aaron Beecham.

For a small town cop, he seemed to be on duty more than off. Okay, that wasn't entirely true. It was just that when he was off duty, the Glass Dolphin was usually open, and she couldn't exactly close the shop for a date. Emily was a fast study, but she had a lot to learn. If a customer came in with a question—

"I should get going," Levon said, interrupting her thoughts. "Gilly is driving around the course checking that everything's perfect before everyone heads out to their respective holes. Once she's back at the clubhouse, I'll do a final drive about. She's relying on me."

I'm sure she is. "I better get going as well. You know what Emily's like about punctuality. If I'm so much as five seconds late, she'll start to panic that we'll be banished from the tournament, or worse, that we won't get to our hole in time. We're starting on number two."

"Just remember not to hit the ball until the shotgun sounds."

"Gilly's using an actual shotgun? I thought everyone used sirens or horns these days."

Levon laughed. "Gilly's as much of a stickler for research as you are. She read back issues of Golf Digest at the library. In 1956 the head pro at the Walla Walla Country Club in Washington—the state, not the city—fired a shotgun into the air to sound the start of play. Apparently that was the first time, though other tournaments have done it since. Gilly thought it would be more authentic if she used a shotgun, too. You of all people should appreciate that, Arabella. After all, isn't that your motto? 'Authenticity matters?'"

It was, but Arabella didn't like that Gilly had adopted the same motto. She didn't like it one bit.

3

ARABELLA MADE her way to the parking lot where the double row of golf carts, equipped with golf bags, were waiting to be driven to their respective holes. One golf cart was missing, which seemed odd, but there was still a good thirty minutes to go before the tournament officially started. Naturally, Emily was already there.

"Poppy Spencer donated golf balls with her real estate logo on them," Emily said by way of greeting. "Every golfer gets a sleeve of three. They're in the cart."

"Good advertising. Even if you lose the ball, someone else will find it and notice the logo."

And it was much more sensible than a jet ski. Why hadn't they thought about golf balls?

Most of the golfers were milling about, checking their phones, chatting, and sampling the coffee, fruit, and breakfast pastries arranged on a side table. Arabella grabbed a lemon poppy seed muffin. "Where are Luke and Hudson?"

"They're here. Luke wanted to check out the jet ski one more time, so he took the cart." She grinned. "I don't think that's in the Gilly Germaine rule book, but she wasn't around to stop him. Neither was Course Marshal Levon."

That would explain the missing cart, Arabella thought, alternately worried and amused at Gilly's potential reaction if or when she found out. "What about Hudson?"

"He's checking out the silent auction table. He donated a signed first edition of his first two books, and a 'name-a-character' in his next book."

Hudson Tanaka was Luke's best friend; an athletic forty-something guy that Emily obviously thought was a good fit for Arabella. Since her split with Aaron, and Levon taking up with Gilly, Emily's not-so-subtle matchmaking attempts had been relentless. Tall, short, fat, thin, if the men were old enough to shave and remotely interested in the opposite sex, Emily seemed to think Arabella would be interested.

Emily was wrong. It wasn't that the men she'd "found" for Arabella were losers. Far from it: they were well educated with decent jobs, or at least a reliable source of income. Hudson Tanaka was a Toronto transplant who had settled in Lakeside to write his third novel. The first two books in his Medieval Knight mystery series apparently sold well enough to afford him a lakefront property. Not in the nosebleed section of Moore Gate Manor, but certainly beyond anything Arabella could hope to afford in this lifetime or the next.

Hudson was also handsome in a storybook sort of way; his slender six-foot frame, long narrow face, and angular chin inherited from his Scandinavian mother—a former magazine and runway model according to Emily—and almond-shaped eyes with the sparkle of black Alaskan diamonds from his Japanese father.

It wasn't his appearance or his profession that was the problem. It was just that Arabella had sworn off men, at least for the time being. Her marriage to Levon had flopped and her relationship with Aaron—which had seemed promising for a while—had been a bust. The last thing she needed was a third strike in the relationship department. She intended to celebrate her upcoming fortieth birthday unattached and proud of it.

A shot rang out, loud and clear. Arabella jumped at the sound. "That must be the starter's gun. Levon said Gilly was going to use a real shotgun." She glanced at her watch. "Talk about a keener. She's a good twenty-five minutes ahead of schedule."

"Maybe she's doing a trial run."

"Seriously," Arabella said. "It's bad enough she's using a real shotgun when the rest of the world is satisfied with a horn. She has to shoot the darned thing twice?"

Emily grinned at her in that way she had when she'd figured out something you didn't necessarily want her to know.

"I'm just saying," Arabella said, knowing that she sounded peevish. "Just saying what?" Hudson appeared at her side.

"Arabella is annoyed that Gilly is using a real shotgun."

"Well, it is a shotgun start," Hudson said, smiling. "Besides, we all know what a perfectionist Gilly is. No detail too small."

"Sounds like someone else I know," Emily said.

Arabella gave her friend an imaginary middle finger. "I'm probably just on edge. I'm not a very good golfer. Actually, 'not very good' would be a compliment."

"Don't be so hard on yourself," Hudson said. "This is a fun tournament for a great cause. Besides, it's best ball."

"I'm not even sure what that means."

"Every cart has a copy of the rules clipped onto the steering wheel. Plus Gilly is bound to go over them before we head out."

A golf cart pulled in and now there was a tidy double row of eighteen carts.

"There's Luke now, arriving in the nick of time, ear buds in as usual," Emily said, but her tone was affectionate.

Gilly came out of the clubhouse, her face flushed. Arabella had to admit that Gilly was stunning in her cool, cultured, and corporate-looking getup. She held a cordless mic in one hand and a piece of paper in the other. She thanked everyone for coming and then turned her attention to the paper.

"Welcome to the Second Annual Kids Come First Golf Tournament. The rules are simple. Each golfer will take a tee shot. The best shot, as determined by all members, will be where each golfer will take their second shot, and so on until you putt out and finish the hole. Please keep pace of play in mind. We have a silent auction with plenty of wonderful items for you to bid on, and lunch will be served promptly at one fifteen. Levon Larroquette will be the Course Marshal." She smiled, the flush receding when Levon appeared.

"Ah, here he is now. He'll be taking you to your respective holes. Please make your way to your carts, and remember not to start until you hear the shotgun."

"I thought I already heard a shotgun," Arabella said. A few other golfers nodded.

Gilly's ice-blue eyes turned icier as she stared Arabella down. "Impossible. The shotgun is locked up in the clubhouse. You must have heard a car backfiring. The road is only a few yards off the parking lot, after all, and people tend to speed along there without any regard for the posted limit. Now pitter-patter let's get at her, shall we? It wouldn't do to start late."

"Why do I feel like saluting?" Arabella muttered, but no one was listening. She marched silently to the golf cart she was sharing with Emily while conflicting thoughts ran through her head. Car backfiring, indeed. She'd heard enough gunfire when she was a kid growing up on a farm to know what it sounded like. That sound had been a shotgun, but who had pulled the trigger? Good luck to Levon, if he was hooked up with Miss Trigger-Happy.

4

EVEN THOUGH SHE was waiting for the sound, the blast from the shotgun made Arabella jump. "That was the shotgun," Luke said.

"Are you sure it's not a car backfiring?" Arabella said, eliciting a chuckle from Emily and Hudson. Luke, however, didn't appear to be amused.

"Remember, silence is golden on the tee." Luke smiled, but Arabella could tell he was serious.

Hudson raised his eyebrows ever so slightly, pulled his driver out of his bag, and walked, ball and tee in hand, ready to hit.

Both men's tee shots were impressive; long and straight down the middle of the fairway. They carted it down to the red advanced tees. Emily hit first. It was another decent shot—not the distance of Luke and Hudson, but a solid one hundred fifty yards. By this time, Arabella was getting anxious. Golf wasn't her thing. She'd only taken it up this spring at Emily's urging and hadn't quite gotten the hang of it. Never an athlete, Arabella was the kid everyone had picked last for any sort of sports team, and for good reason.

She walked over to the tee box, silently cursing Emily, and tried to remember everything that Robbie Andrews, the Head Pro at the Miakoda Falls Golf and Country Club, had taught her in her weekly lessons. Robbie was nicknamed "The Saint"—a nod to the prestigious St. Andrews Golf Course in Scotland and Robbie's reputation as an infinitely patient instructor. But even Robbie's tolerant temperament had been tested by Arabella's inability to grasp the basics.

She took a deep breath, determined to get it right. Feet slightly wider than shoulders. Left foot slightly turned out. The ball just inside her left heel. She gripped the club lightly, her fingers interlaced the way Robbie had instructed, and looked for two V's formed by her thumbs and index fingers. She took another deep breath and a practice swing followed by one more swing for good measure. Finally hitting the ball, Arabella watched it go about fifty yards and land in a sand trap shaped like Mickey Mouse ears.

"I'm sorry."

"Relax," Hudson said. "It's best ball, and we're here to support Kids Come First. Don't stress yourself."

Emily gave Arabella a look that said, "See, I told you he was a good guy."

"Hudson's right," Luke said. "This is supposed to be fun. Let's go see which ball we're going to use. We can pick up the other balls along the way."

The rest of the hole wasn't much better, even though everyone made a big deal about how Arabella's putting saved the team a stroke. She had to admit that all those visits to the mini putt when she was growing up were coming in handy.

Arabella had to admit that arriving at the third hole and seeing the jet ski on display was exciting. A man wearing a Toronto Blue Jays baseball cap and blue and black plaid pants sat in a chair behind the tee box and off to the left side. He nodded, but didn't speak.

"He's from the hole in one insurance company," Emily said, stating the obvious. "They told me they were going to send someone. I suppose they're worried someone might try to cheat."

The thought of someone cheating hadn't even occurred to Arabella, which was just as well. She'd had enough sleepless nights over this jet ski business.

Once again, she let the others go first. All three managed to clear the pond and land on the green, but no one was anywhere close to getting a hole in one. Arabella breathed a sigh of relief; they might not be eligible to win, but it still freaked her out to think someone else might. She went through her mental prep, took her swing, and watched her ball veer directly into the woods.

"Hey, you made it over the water," Hudson said, hopping into his cart. "For someone just starting out, that's not a bad shot."

Arabella caught Emily's look and smiled. He really was a nice guy. "Thanks, Hudson. Whether I can find my ball is an entirely different story. Why don't I look for it while you guys putt in? I'm sure one of you will be able to get it in the hole."

They crossed the pond on a wooden bridge just wide enough for their golf carts, parked on the path next to the hole, and grabbed their putters. Luke, Hudson, and Emily walked to the green and began debating which ball to hit. Arabella trundled over to the woods, feeling stupid and hoping like hell it wasn't infested with poison ivy. The woods were thicker than she'd expected. She walked in a couple of feet, using her putter to push the branches aside.

That's when she started to scream.

5

ARABELLA HAD NEARLY TRIPPED over the body of a man, mid-to-late sixties. Based on his physique—long and lean—he'd either been fit or blessed with a great metabolism. She pulled herself together and leaned down to take his pulse, knowing full well she wouldn't find one. The hole in his chest was her first clue. The second was the cloudy film over his sightless blue eyes. She had no idea how long he'd been dead, but his wrist was still warmish to the touch. She resisted the urge to close his eyes.

Arabella stood up to find Luke, Hudson, and Emily standing behind her, their eyes wide, mouths gaping open. The guy from the insurance company was running across the bridge, a piece of paper flapping in his hand. Luke pulled his cell phone out of his pocket. "Gilly," he said, his voice tense, "there's a problem at the third hole. You need to call off the tournament. Get Levon and whomever else you can summon up to ride out to the other holes and gather everyone back into the clubhouse. Do not take them by the third hole. I repeat, do not take them by the third hole. Make sure nobody leaves. I'll get the police here."

There was a moment of silence after Luke made his announcement to Gilly. Arabella strained her ears to try to pick up what she was rambling about on her end. Probably trying to figure out if it was really necessary to call off the tournament, Arabella thought once she heard Luke speak again. "Yes, it's definitely a matter for the police. Sound the horn, the one you'd use if there were a threat of lightning. Our foursome will do our best to secure the area. You do the rest."

Y

THE FIVE OF them stood awkwardly, not quite sure of what to say or where to look. Fortunately, Luke took on the role of leader of the pack, shepherding them away from the body toward their golf carts. After a couple of minutes, the insurance guy, who introduced himself as Trent Norland, started the conversation. He kept fidgeting with the sheet of paper as he spoke.

"To think I was sitting here all this time with a dead body only a few yards away. I hope the police don't think I had anything to do with it."

"I'm sure they won't," Luke said.

Arabella wasn't so sure. She figured they'd all be persons of interest, at least initially. But she wasn't about to say so. The group fell silent again.

The wait for the police seemed endless, at least for Arabella, though in truth it was less than ten minutes before Constable Aaron Beecham and Detective Sheridan Merryfield arrived on the scene.

It had been about a month since Arabella had seen Aaron. The first thing she noticed was that he'd lost weight, and a lot of it. He'd always been what could best be described as burly. Now, however, he was borderline gaunt, which was made all the more obvious as he stood next to Merryfield—a tall man with skin the color of Kraft caramels, biceps that strained the sleeves of his shirt, and hands the size of goalie gloves.

"Aaron," she said. She wanted to reach out and hug him, tell him she'd missed him, ask if he was okay, but it wasn't the appropriate place or time.

"Arabella, Luke said you're the one who found the body." All business. Not even a hint of a smile in his gray-blue eyes.

She swallowed hard and pointed to the wooded area. "My ball went into the trees." Merryfield's gaze focused on the woods, and then back to Arabella. "Go on."

"I was rooting around for my ball using my putter. I was afraid there might be poison ivy. I've had it before and…and it doesn't matter. That's when I found the body."

"Did you touch anything?" Merryfield asked.

"I took his pulse. There wasn't one. That's when I noticed the hole in his chest. Or maybe I noticed the hole in his chest before and tried to take his pulse anyway. It's a blur. But the surrounding area, I know I didn't touch that, except with my putter, of course."

"Did anyone else touch anything?"

Emily, Luke, Hudson, and Trent shook their heads in unison.

"We were putting when we heard Arabella scream," Emily said.

"I was sitting beside the tee box," Trent said, gesturing toward the chair. "Trent Norland. I'm with the company providing the hole in one insurance. For the jet ski? People cheat. I'm here to make sure they don't."

Merryfield nodded and made his way over to the body. "Looks like a single gunshot wound to the chest," Merryfield said quietly, addressing Beecham. "Someone from the coroner's office will be here any minute. See if our murderer left any clues. It would be nice if he left the gun behind."

Beecham slipped on a pair of gloves and trod gingerly into the woods. Merryfield turned his attention to Trent.

"How long were you sitting there by yourself before the first group arrived?"

Trent flushed under Merryfield's gaze. "Ten minutes, maybe fifteen. I didn't see anyone or anything suspicious."

"Who was in the first foursome?"

Trent referred to the sheet of paper he'd been holding. "Poppy Spencer, Chantal Van Schyndle, Ned Turcotte, and Miles Pemberton. None of them hit their ball anywhere near the woods."

Arabella knew Poppy, of course. Chantal owned the Serenity

Spa and Yoga Studio, and Ned was the owner of Birdsong. Both shops were on Main Street in Lount's Landing, near the Glass Dolphin, but she'd never heard of Miles Pemberton. She cast a quick glance at Emily, who gave an almost imperceptible shake of her head.

"Did anyone hear a gunshot?" Beecham asked.

"It's a shotgun tournament," Luke said. "Gilly Germaine—that's the tournament organizer—used a real shotgun. So we did hear a shot."

"Actually, we heard two shots," Arabella said. "The first shot was about twenty-five minutes before Levon drove us out to our respective holes. I remember thinking it was overkill." She blushed. "Sorry, bad choice of words. What I meant was, Gilly is very... detail oriented. I assumed she'd taken a practice shot, but when I asked her about it at the rules briefing, she said it was impossible, that the shotgun was locked up in the clubhouse. She thought it was a car backfiring."

"I didn't hear it, but I had my ear buds in listening to tunes," Luke said.

"It could have been a car backfiring," Hudson said. "Or a shot from a shotgun," Arabella shot back.

Emily's eyes brightened. "Do you think one shot might have been the one to start the tournament, and the other shot killed—" Merryfield's look stopped her cold.

"Ladies, and by that I mean you, Emily Garland, and you, Arabella Carpenter. Let me make one thing perfectly clear. You are not, I repeat, not to start investigating this. You were lucky to come out of your last investigation alive, and we don't have the manpower or the patience to babysit you."

Arabella knew Emily missed her job as an investigative reporter. But this was different from their last case. It wasn't like they had any connection to the dead man. Except...

"There's something vaguely familiar about him," Arabella said, her brow furrowed in concentration.

"Familiar how?" Merryfield asked.

"I can't put a finger on it. Does anyone else get the same feeling?"

"Can't say as I do," Hudson said. "I'm positive I've never seen this man before in my life." Luke frowned and shook his head.

Trent followed suit.

"I don't recognize him. Maybe he came into the Glass Dolphin when I wasn't there," Emily offered.

"No, it isn't that. I make it a point to remember customers." Arabella was still trying to figure it out when Levon rode up in his golf cart, the black and gold Marshal flag flapping. He pulled up next to the green.

"Everyone is being escorted back to the clubhouse. Gilly is in a major league snit over this. She claims her reputation will be irreversibly tarnished——" Levon's voice trailed off as he caught sight of the body, his face ghostly pale beneath his tan.

"Do you know this man?" Merryfield asked.

"It's been a few years, twenty-four to be exact. But yes, I'd recognize him anywhere. His name is Marc Larroquette."

Arabella let out an involuntary gasp, tried to stifle it, didn't quite succeed.

"Marc Larroquette. A relative of yours, then." Aaron Beecham's eyes flicked from Arabella to Levon to Arabella and back again.

"You could say that," Levon said. "The last time I saw him he was going out to get a pack of smokes. I was fifteen at the time. You see, this man is…was…my father. My long-lost father. And until now, I haven't been missing him."

6

ARABELLA WAS sure Levon was lying. Perhaps not about Marc Larroquette being his father, because there was a strong physical resemblance between the two. But Levon had seen Marc recently. She had seen Levon arguing with the dead man a couple of days before.

She'd been walking through the park when she'd heard Levon's voice, low, but tinged with simmering, barely controlled anger. She saw him and the man she now knew as Marc Larroquette semi-hidden in the wooded area behind the main pathway. Arabella had reversed her route to slip away unnoticed. The last thing she needed was Levon thinking that she was following him.

But if she had seen Levon with Marc, then others might have as well. In fact, in a town the size of Lount's Landing, it was pretty much guaranteed.

Maybe Levon was worried that he'd be suspected of murder if the truth got out. Though Levon was promising to help the police in any way possible, what if the police caught him in a lie?

Arabella knew something the police didn't. When the police were talking to Levon, he took his sunglasses off and gently rubbed his right eye. Maybe Merryfield and Beecham would think he had allergies, but Arabella knew her ex rubbed his right eye when he was lying.

For the moment, the police appeared to accept Levon's explanation, although Arabella knew there would be plenty of other questions to come—for all of them.

Merryfield told them to make their way back to the clubhouse and await further instructions. He stared long and hard at Levon as he said, "Constable Beecham will follow behind to make certain that no one gets lost along the way."

Arabella knew then that Levon was a suspect. His pained expression showed he knew it, too.

🍸

THE SILENCE in the Bogey Ballroom of the Miakoda Falls Golf and Country Club was palpable. Incredible, given all thirty-six golfers were in attendance. It looked like everyone had stayed with their foursomes and Arabella followed suit, taking a seat at a table with Emily, Luke, and Hudson. Trent joined them, looking decidedly like a guy who wanted to be anywhere but here. Horseshoe bald, he was almost unrecognizable without the Blue Jays baseball cap, but the plaid pants were a dead giveaway. What was it about golf that made plaid pants seem like a good fashion choice?

She scanned the room for Levon and saw him sitting alone at the back of the room, his gaze averted, shoulders slumped forward. She recognized Constable Sarah Byrne, a recent recruit to the Cedar County Tri-Community Policing Center, affectionately known by locals as the One-Tric-Pokey.

Arabella had met Sarah a few months earlier at a "Welcome Rookie" barbecue hosted by Detective Merryfield, with Aaron Beecham as her date. The day of the party, Sarah had worn white capris, a blue and white cropped tee shirt, and a hint of makeup, her strawberry blonde hair hanging loose in soft waves that barely brushed the top of her bare shoulders. Today, Sarah's face was devoid of makeup, her hair had been pulled back into a French braid, and her police uniform of black pants, black shirt, and black vest bulked up her trim figure.

Arabella continued looking around the room. Based on the stunned look on people's faces, she figured they knew about the basic situation.

Gilly Germaine looked positively green, her eyes darting from person to person, eventually landing on Levon. She started to walk toward him but stopped when he looked up, shook his head, and re-averted his gaze. Her lower lip trembled a bit, but she carefully hid her disappointment—or was it confusion?

Arabella thought no one else was paying enough attention to notice.

She was wrong. Aaron's blue-gray eyes were assessing both Gilly and Levon.

Every move Levon made was being closely monitored. Heck, every move she made was probably being closely monitored too. She was the one who'd found the dead body of her ex-husband's allegedly long-lost father. Maybe the police would think she and Levon had been in on it together. Or would they? Surely Aaron wouldn't suspect her?

A microphone crackled. The golfers murmured to one another and shuffled their chairs to face the side of the room where Merryfield, Beecham, and Byrne stood shoulder-to-shoulder. Gilly sat at a table off to their left, her posture unnaturally rigid, as if willing herself not to cry. As much as Gilly annoyed her, Arabella couldn't help but feel sorry for the woman. Levon said the tournament had been Gilly's all-consuming project. She'd put hours of hard work organizing the tournament and arranging for silent auction donations.

Merryfield's voice quieted the murmurs and stilled the shuffles of chairs. He licked his lips quickly, a flick of the tip of his tongue. It was a habit Arabella had observed when he'd interviewed her last year. That had been another murder. She shivered, even though the room was warm, the air conditioning struggling against the heat outside, and the packed house inside.

"Thank you all for your cooperation," Merryfield said. "While we cannot stop you from discussing this after you leave here, we ask that you use discretion. Please do not resort to gossip or embellish the facts. In that spirit, Constable Beecham will update you on what we have learned so far."

Aaron Beecham cleared his throat and took the mic. Arabella was struck again by how much weight he had lost since she'd seen him last. Had their breakup affected him physically?

"At approximately nine-fifteen this morning, one of the golfers in the tournament hit a ball into the wooded area adjacent to hole number three," Beecham began. "While searching for the ball, the golfer discovered the body of a man. An investigation is underway. Constable Byrne and I will conduct individual interviews in the Eagle Lounge. Once your contact information has been recorded and your interview completed, we ask that you leave the premises. We do, however, reserve the right to speak with you again in the future, should the need arise. Are there any questions?"

Gilly raised her hand. "I realize this sounds insensitive, but what about lunch and the silent auction?"

"The silent auction will have to be postponed," Merryfield said. "Since it will take some time to interview everyone, lunch would be a good idea. But I'd like to keep the movements of the kitchen staff to a minimum."

"We have trays of assorted sandwiches, salads, and desserts prepped for each table," Gilly said. "I'll ask for the food to be set up on a banquet table instead, buffet-style, along with coffee, tea, and water."

"Thank you, Gilly, that's an excellent solution. Are there any other questions?"

A few folks raised their hands. A tall, reed-thin brunette stood up. Unlike the rest of the people in the room, she wasn't dressed in golf attire. The woman wore a floral sundress in muted shades of pink and purple, and glasses with thick-rimmed frames that matched. Not beautiful, at least not in the traditional sense, but oddly compelling. Luke, Hudson, and Trent were staring at the woman as if transfixed.

"Oh for cripes sake," Emily muttered, her face flushed with displeasure. "What the hell is Kerri Say-no-more doing here?"

"She's probably here to cover the tournament for the paper," Arabella whispered, hoping Emily wouldn't make a scene. She knew her friend was still sensitive about being terminated by *Inside the Landing*. Being replaced by Kerri, a woman she'd previously had a combative relationship with back in Toronto, had been almost too much to bear.

"One person at a time, please," Beecham said, shooting a warning glance in Arabella and Emily's direction. Emily's flush deepened, and the scowl on her face looked as if it might become permanently ingrained.

"The woman in the floral dress. Please state your name and your question."

"Kerri St. Amour, editor of *Inside the Landing*. Do you know the identity of the dead man?"

"Yes, but we are unable to make his identity public at this time. Are there any other questions?" Beecham's eyes scanned the room. Kerri St. Amour remained standing. With no other hands raised, he turned his attention back to the reporter. "Ms. St. Amour?"

"You said that a golfer had discovered the body, but you didn't say who that individual was. Can you share that information with us?"

"Not at this time."

"But we know, don't we, that the gentleman providing the hole in one insurance, Trent Norland, would have been present. Surely we can determine, quite easily, which group would have been at the third hole. By my calculations, the group in question would have included Arabella Carpenter, Hudson Tanaka, Luke Surmanski— and Emily Garland."

Was it Arabella's imagination, or had Kerri put an emphasis on Emily's name? She glanced at Emily, taking in the angry splotches of red on her face. Nope, definitely not her imagination. First Levon, now Emily. Something told her this was about to get a whole lot uglier.

7

EMILY GARLAND SEETHED SILENTLY. The nerve of that vulture, implying that she was somehow involved in the death of Marc Larroquette. She didn't know anything about the murder, but she was certain it would only be a matter of time before Kerri, the grubby bloodhound, would find out and leak the news, implicating her and Arabella. The Glass Dolphin would make headlines—for all the wrong reasons. That Kerri didn't know the dead man's name, or his relationship to Levon, was small comfort.

Emily took a deep breath and forced herself to calm down. Fortunately, Aaron Beecham wasn't capitulating to Kerri's line of questioning, and Merryfield seemed annoyed by it. The rookie, Sarah Byrne, looked a bit lost. She'd probably thought coming to Cedar County would be an easy ride. No such luck. After last year's string of murders, and now this, Emily figured the county was cursed.

No one else had questions, likely figuring that if a reporter couldn't get answers, they wouldn't either. Or maybe they just wanted to get back to the safety of their own homes. As far as golf tournaments went, this one didn't make the cut.

Beecham announced that they would get started on the

interviews. Last names starting with A through L were to stay put in the Bogey Ballroom, and he'd call each name in alphabetical order. Names M through Z should relocate to the Eagle Lounge where Detective Merryfield would be in charge. Officer Byrne would be checking everyone's golf bag and cart. No one was to leave until each golf bag was thoroughly checked.

Trent Norland left their table without a word. Luke and Hudson assured Emily and Arabella they would get together "soon" and followed Trent to the Eagle Lounge.

Emily figured their idea of "soon" and hers might be different. Damn. She was just getting to really know—and like—Luke, and she'd really hoped that Hudson and Arabella might hit it off, too. She also wondered if the alphabetical split was made that way so Aaron could take on Levon Larroquette. It seemed like Arabella was thinking the same thing. There was no love lost between Levon and Aaron, even though both of them were no longer involved romantically with Arabella.

It already looked bad for Levon. Even though Emily couldn't speak for the police, she'd bet money that Arabella wasn't buying that Levon hadn't seen his father in years—not that she'd ever admit it. When it came to Levon, Arabella's judgment was clouded.

Emily scanned the half-empty room and found Levon hunched over a table at the back, staring at his hands. He glanced up as if he felt her staring at him, nodded in acknowledgment without so much as a flicker of a smile, and then resumed his former position. Was he grief-stricken, guilty, or both?

"Arabella Carpenter," Beecham called. Emily patted Arabella on the leg and leaned in to whisper. "It will be over before you know it."

Arabella nodded and followed Beecham through a door marked PRIVATE. Emily thought she looked like a woman going to her own execution. She was hiding something. Emily knew it. But what? Surely she hadn't known there was a dead body in the woods. Or had she?

Of course she hadn't. And neither had Levon. Emily gave

herself a mental slap on the head. These were her friends. They weren't Bonnie and Clyde, a pair of killers in cahoots.

But Arabella said she had recognized the body, or at least thought he looked familiar. Was it the resemblance to her ex-husband? Once you knew the connection, it was easy enough to spot, but Emily was certain there was more to it than that.

She mulled over the possibilities. What if Levon had seen his father recently, and not twenty-some years ago as he had told the police? What if he'd told Arabella? No, that wouldn't work. The two of them hadn't talked much since Gilly Germaine had arrived on the scene—a fact that Emily knew bothered Arabella more than she was willing to admit.

But what if Arabella had seen Levon and his father together, somewhere off the beaten path? What if Levon didn't know Arabella had seen him?

Emily nodded. That was the most plausible explanation; she was sure of it.

Which meant Levon was lying, Arabella was covering up for him, and Emily was going to be dragged into trying to clear his name.

8

ARABELLA SAT across from Aaron Beecham in the Head Pro's closet-sized office. It felt claustrophobic, but it was no doubt meant to ensure that Robbie Andrews spent most of his time in the pro shop mingling and chatting up the customers, versus sitting inside doing paperwork. Based on the untidy stack of files in his inbox, the strategy was working.

"You've lost a lot of weight," Arabella said, aware this might not be the time to bring it up, but concerned enough to risk it.

The expression on Aaron's face was a mix of amusement and annoyance. "I've been trying out a vegan diet."

A vegan diet? Was this the same guy who'd taken her out for steak and ribs on their first date? She suppressed a sigh. It was bad enough that Emily was a vegetarian, though at least she'd eat eggs and dairy. A "lacto-ovo" vegetarian, Emily called it, and then had gone on to explain the different levels of vegetarianism. Vegans, Arabella remembered, didn't even eat honey, considering it an animal byproduct.

"Sarah Byrne got me into it," Aaron said. "I must say I feel better, though I'll admit I miss cheeseburgers. I've tried veggie burgers, and they're just not the same. And that soy cheese should be outlawed."

Sarah Byrne? Was something going on between Beecham and the rookie officer?

"We're just friends and co-workers, Arabella," Aaron said, reading her mind. "Now, let's focus on the issue at hand. The death of Marc Larroquette."

"I've already told you everything I know."

"Humor me."

What happened to the guy she'd almost fallen in love with? The one who once cared about what she thought and how she felt? She understood that Aaron had to be professional, but would it kill him to show a hint of compassion? It wasn't like she found a dead body every day.

She bit back a snarky reply, knowing it would come back to haunt her—or Levon. She could deal with whatever Aaron dished out, but she couldn't risk it hurting her ex-husband.

"I hit my tee shot into the trees on the third hole. I went to look for my ball while the others were putting. I was worried there might be poison ivy in the woods, so I was rooting around for the ball with my putter. I hit something and noticed it was a shoe…I'd nearly tripped over the body…and I started to scream."

"Go on."

"I leaned down to check for a pulse. That was wrong, I know. I shouldn't have touched him, especially since I could tell the man was dead. But it was an instinctive reaction. I hope I didn't mess up the scene."

If Arabella was hoping for absolution, she didn't get it. "What happened next?"

"I stood up. Luke, Emily, and Hudson were standing there. I think the guy from the insurance company, Trent Norland, came a couple of seconds later, but he would have had to run from the tee box and across the bridge." Arabella paused. She hadn't thought about it earlier, but from his vantage point, would Trent have been able to see the body?

"Go on," Beecham said, again.

"Right. Sorry. Someone—I'm pretty sure it was Luke—called Gilly and told her to stop the tournament and get everyone to the clubhouse. Then he called the police."

"Did Luke mention the body when he called Gilly Germaine?"

Arabella closed her eyes a minute, trying to recall Luke's words. "No, I'm positive he didn't. He just said something along the lines of 'it's serious.' I had the impression Gilly didn't want to stop the tournament. He told her it was important and to sound the lightning horn."

"Did you see Levon Larroquette anywhere?"

Damn. So her instincts were right. They considered Levon to be a suspect. "I saw him earlier at the silent auction table. That was at least an hour before the tournament started. I didn't see him on the course until after you arrived. He was acting as the Course Marshal."

"So, you didn't know where he was."

"Asked and answered."

Beecham rolled his eyes. "I apologize if the questions seem repetitive to you, Arabella, but this isn't an episode of Law and Order. I'm going to ask you again. Did you know where Levon was?"

Arabella felt like a chastised schoolgirl, and she resented Aaron for making her feel that way. He knew her—she wasn't the kind of person to lie. If anything, her penchant for honesty and integrity above all else is what got her into hot water. Then again, when it came to Levon even her exacting principles could be bent a little. He knew that, too.

"I did not see Levon again until he rode up to the third hole. You and Merryfield were already there."

"I believe you."

"Thank you," she said with exaggerated gratitude. Aaron ignored the effort. "You said that the dead man looked familiar. In what way?"

Double damn. That was the thing about always telling the truth. It turned you into a terrible liar. She forced herself to maintain eye contact and shrugged nonchalantly. "I suppose it could have been because he reminded me of Levon."

"It could have been, but that wasn't the reason, was it?"

Bastard. "No."

"I'm listening."

"I was walking in the park a couple of days ago when I noticed Levon talking to a man I didn't know. I don't think either one of them saw me. I didn't realize, at the time, that the man with him was his father. I'd never met Marc Larroquette, and I'd never seen a photograph."

"You were married to Levon. Do you expect me to believe you'd never seen a photograph of his father?"

Arabella bristled. "Believe what you want."

Beecham colored slightly. "Did you hear what they were talking about in the park?"

"I'm not an eavesdropper. I turned around the moment I spotted them."

"Were they arguing?"

"Yes. They were in the wooded area behind the path."

Beecham raised his eyebrows ever so slightly, but didn't comment.

"Listen, Levon and I haven't spoken much lately. He's been dating Gilly Germaine."

Was that a look of surprise or amusement on Beecham's face?

"I didn't want him to think I'd been stalking him." She paused. "Is there anything else, Constable Beecham, or do you want to subject me to further humiliation?"

"I'm not trying to humiliate you, Arabella. A murder has been committed. Your personal feelings for Levon factor into the equation, whether you like it or not."

Arabella knew he was right. "I'm sorry. Is there anything else?"

"Just one more question. Were Levon and his father estranged?"

"Yes. His father walked out on him and his mom when Levon was a teenager. He went out for a pack of cigarettes and never came back. No warning, no notice, no reason."

"That must have been hard on Levon and his mother."

"You'd have to ask Levon. All I know is what he told me. That he hadn't seen or heard from him since."

"Until two days ago in the park, where they were arguing," Beecham said. "And now Marc Larroquette is dead."

9

Arabella and Emily were back at the Glass Dolphin by three o'clock. A sign on the door said "Closed for the Day."

"I suppose we could open," Arabella said, without enthusiasm.

Emily slipped off her sandals and flopped into a press back rocking chair. Everything in the shop was for sale, but that didn't stop them from using the furniture. It was part of Arabella's sales strategy to demonstrate that the things on display were meant to be employed and enjoyed in day-to-day life, not treated like objects in a museum. From Emily's perspective, opening would mean checking the website stats, monitoring their eBay listings, and maybe listing a few more smalls, like the perfume bottles Arabella had found in Pottageville. While she was debating this, the doorbell chimed, announcing a customer. Kerri St. Amour flounced in, her eyes scanning the premises from top to bottom.

"What part of 'closed for the day' don't you understand?" Emily asked, her tone acerbic.

"I tried the door. It was unlocked. If you didn't want anyone coming in, you should have locked it."

"We don't want anyone pilfering anything, either, but we don't feel the need to hang up a sign saying, 'No stealing.' Some things are just understood. At least by anyone with a moral compass."

Arabella saw Kerri flinch. She'd never found out exactly why Emily disliked her so much, but she knew it went far deeper than Kerri moving to Lount's Landing to take over the editorial gig at *Inside the Landing*. Something had happened back in Toronto when they were both freelancing for Urban Living.

"I think what Emily is trying to say is why pay us a visit now?" Arabella said, hands on her hips, a "don't mess with me" expression on her face. "You've been in Lount's Landing for the better part of six months. In all that time, you've never once stepped foot inside the shop."

"Okay, fine, you've got me there. I'm here about the body your group found today. It's newsworthy, and I run a newspaper. I have a responsibility to my readers to report the news."

"Fabricate the news is more like it," Emily muttered under her breath.

Kerri had changed the format and frequency of *Inside the Landing* from a monthly magazine to a weekly newspaper. It appeared to be doing well; one more sore point for Emily, but this was no time for a catfight. The last thing she wanted was Kerri building a case against one of them. Guilty or innocent, once an accusation was public, reputations were forever tarnished. She also knew that Kerri was venomous enough to target Levon if it meant hurting them.

"I'm afraid we can't tell you anything," Arabella said, shooting Emily a warning glance. "Detective Merryfield and Constable Beecham made it very clear we weren't to discuss it, as you well know since you were at the briefing. We wouldn't want to get into trouble with the police. I'm sure you understand."

Kerri laughed, a harsh, guttural sound that gave Arabella the shivers. "Is that why you think I'm here? To find out what you know?"

"Well, isn't it?" Arabella asked.

"Actually, I'm here to tell you what I know. Detective Merryfield was more than happy to meet with me after everyone had been interviewed. He thinks that reporting selected details in the paper might encourage people to come forward with additional information that could potentially solve the case."

"What sort of selected details?" Arabella asked.

"The body has been positively identified as Marc Larroquette. Larroquette, as in Levon. It seems Marc was Levon's father, although from what Merryfield told me, the two were long estranged. But I assume you both already knew that." Kerri paused, a half smile playing on her lips. "What you don't know is that Levon has been taken into police custody. The way I figure it, it's just a matter of time until he's charged with murder."

Arabella fought the urge to claw Kerri's eyes out. Don't shoot the messenger, even when the messenger was trying to mess with your head. She swallowed, picked up a Baccarat millefiori paperweight and rubbed the glass to calm her nerves. "No comment."

"No comment from me, either," Emily said, standing up. "I think you've overstayed your welcome here, Kerri. It would be best if you left. Now."

Kerri shrugged. "Have it your way, ladies. The story is going to run with your comments or without them. I just thought you'd have something to add, seeing that Levon is Arabella's ex- husband."

"My relationship with Levon is irrelevant," Arabella said. "Is it? I guess we'll find out soon enough, won't we?"

10

KERRI LEFT before Arabella could throw the paperweight at her, mostly because Emily insisted Arabella put it down. It was priced at a thousand dollars, after all—a reasonable price for a nineteenth-century Baccarat.

Arabella opened a Canadiana pine sideboard, and pulled out a tin of shortbread. The cookies were technically for guests but she needed something to help settle her down. Hopefully the shortbread would do the trick. She offered the tin to Emily, who shook her head. She was on her fourth cookie and starting to feel a bit sick to her stomach, when Emily spoke up.

"Kerri could be making it up. Levon might not be in police custody."

"Maybe. I'd like to believe she was lying."

"According to Levon, he hadn't seen his father in twenty-four years." Arabella stared at her feet.

"What aren't you telling me?"

"If you must know, Levon lied about that. I saw him at the park a couple of days ago. He was arguing with a man who I now realize was Marc Larroquette."

"Hmm. That's not good."

Arabella laughed, a dry, humorless sound. "Ya think?"

"Did you happen to hear what they were arguing about?"

"Just a few words. It was something along the lines of 'leave her out of this.' I have no idea who 'her' is. It could be me, for all I know. Or Gilly. I left before Levon could see me. But—"

"But what?"

"I told Aaron about seeing them together when he interviewed me."

"Did you tell him they were arguing?"

"No, but he figured it out." Tears trickled down Arabella's face. "Oh god, Emily. What if I'm the reason Levon's in custody?"

"You can't blame yourself. The police were bound to find out sooner or later. Lount's Landing is a small town. There had to be others who saw them together."

And those people were the ones who would come forward with more "information" after they read Kerri's article in the paper.

Arabella put the cookies away. No amount of shortbread was going to fix this mess.

Y

EMILY BROUGHT a copy of *Inside the Landing* into the shop the next morning. Arabella wanted to thank her, but the words stuck in her throat when she saw the front page: MURDER IN MIAKODA FALLS. Arabella felt a tug somewhere deep inside her stomach and leaned over to read the story.

The body of a man was found discovered on the third hole of the Miakoda Falls Golf & Country Club during a golf tournament for the children's charity, Kids Come First. The man died from a single gunshot wound to the chest.

Additional details of the death are being withheld at this time, pending notification of next of kin.

However, an exclusive anonymous *Inside the Landing* source has confirmed that the dead man was Marc Larroquette, the estranged father of Levon Larroquette, owner of Larroquette's Antiques Pickers & Appraisers.

"Kerri St. Amour at her finest," Emily said. "She's the queen of rumor and innuendo. Interesting, though, about the next-of-kin. I just assumed Levon was his only living relative."

"Yeah, I guess I did too." Arabella wondered if Levon knew about the next-of-kin. She turned her attention back to the article.

The group playing in the charity tournament that discovered the body included Luke Surmanski, owner of Luke's Lakeside Marina, Hudson Tanaka, author of the Medieval Knight mystery series, and Arabella Carpenter and Emily Garland, co-owners of the Glass Dolphin antiques shop.

Arabella's green eyes filled with rage. "Did she have to name us?"

"Classic Kerri Say-no-more," Emily said. "Read on."

Arabella did. On page three there was a photo that looked like a police artist's sketch, with the caption "Have You Seen This Man?" Arabella studied it briefly, trying to reconcile the drawing with the man she'd seen with Levon. It was a decent likeness, given that the model had been a corpse.

Police suspect that the dead man arrived in Lount's Landing within the past week to ten days. Any person who has seen this man, contact Detective Sheridan Merryfield at 555- 853-5763 to arrange a confidential interview.

"I suppose it could have been worse," Arabella said.

Emily bit her lip. "Actually, it is."

11

ARABELLA STARED AT EMILY. "What do you mean? How can things be worse than what Kerri is insinuating in the paper?"

"Check online," Emily said. "There's a new local blog. The posts are written by 'Truth Seeker,' but I'm positive Kerri is behind it."

"How can you be positive if they're using a pseudonym?"

"It's called *Outside the Landing*."

Truth Seeker. *Outside the Landing*. Arabella wanted to mock the absurdity of it all, but she knew this was no laughing matter. Real lives and hard-earned reputations were at stake. "Catchy."

"Not as catchy as what she's writing on her blog. The headline reads 'WHO IS THE MIAKODA MURDERER?' and the blogger has plenty of factoids to share."

Arabella groaned. "Let me read it. I don't want to be the only one in the Landing to be out of the loop."

Emily pushed her tablet toward Arabella. "Here you go. Don't say I didn't warn you."

The first thing Arabella noticed was the picture of Levon. The photo was about five years old, taken at a charity auction where

Levon had been the auctioneer. They had still been together, barely hanging on to what they had, but trying to get past the stuff that was breaking them up. He looked good, no gray in his shaggy brown hair, the indigo blue eyes clear and guilt-free. She felt a tug somewhere deep inside her stomach and braced herself for the worst.

This blogger has learned folks have been FAST AND FURIOUS in contacting the Miakoda Falls Police Department after *Inside the Landing*'s recent report on the murder of Marc Larroquette. While the police are keeping details under wraps, a little bird told this blogger that Levon and Marc Larroquette were ARGUING in the park before the MURDER.

A prominent local realtor, who has asked to remain ANONYMOUS, has confirmed that she was working with Mr. Larroquette at the time of his death. Could they have been arguing about Marc's decision to BUY A HOME in Lount's Landing?

The prominent local realtor had to be Poppy Spencer, Arabella thought. Had Levon known that his father had been house hunting? If so, how many other things was he hiding? She kept reading.

The realtor went on to say that the senior Larroquette's second wife, Alice, had had been killed four years ago in an automobile accident in Sault Ste. Marie, Ontario. The couple had been legally separated at the time of the crash.

"Marc was haunted by Alice's untimely death and hoped to reconnect with his son," the realtor CONFIDED to *Outside the Landing*.

Did that decision cost Marc his LIFE? Follow this blog for the LATEST scoop.

Arabella resisted the urge to throw the tablet across the room. That action wouldn't solve anything. But what action would?

Any way you sliced it, Levon was in for a world of hurt.

Y

ARABELLA HAD BEEN WAITING for Levon to call. Ironically, when her phone rang later that evening, she wasn't quite sure what to say to him. She was glad, however, that she was away from the shop and at home. As much as she loved Emily, she didn't feel like sharing every conversation with her.

"Have you read the article in *Inside the Landing*?" Levon asked, without preamble. "Hello to you as well, and yes, I read it."

"What about the blog? *Outside the Landing*?"

"Read that one, too. Emily and I think Truth Seeker and Kerri St. Amour are one and the same."

"No argument here."

Arabella paused, wondering how to phrase her next question. She decided to approach it head on. "Did you know your dad was looking at houses?"

"Don't call him my dad. That's a title reserved for men who actually stick around to parent their kids."

"Fine. Your father then. I wondered if you knew your father was looking at houses?"

There was a long silence. So long that Arabella checked her phone to see if the call had been dropped. It hadn't.

"Levon? Did you know—"

There was an audible sigh and then, "Yes. I knew. He actually thought I'd be happy to hear the news. He hired Poppy Spencer. I told him buying here was a poor decision, although maybe not quite that politely. He was adamant. I considered asking Poppy not to represent him, but what good would that do? He'd only find another agent. I stopped at begging him to reconsider his plan, although I'm ashamed to admit the thought crossed my mind. But you know me. I don't beg, even when I know I'm losing someone I love."

It was a not-so-subtle dig at Arabella leaving him when she suspected him of cheating on her. To this day, Levon insisted it was all a big misunderstanding, and while she wanted to be convinced of his innocence, the thought that he'd strayed hurt too much. Even so, she had to do what she could to prove Levon was innocent.

"Maybe there were others that Marc wronged and wanted to make right."

"I wouldn't be surprised."

"Do you have any idea who they might be?"

"No."

Was there a slight hesitation before the 'no?' Arabella thought there had been, but she couldn't be sure, and she knew pushing him would get her nowhere.

She wondered where Marc Larroquette had planned to relocate from and why, but Levon often had a three-question policy. Ask too many questions and he'd just stop answering. It was one of his more annoying habits.

She thought hard before formulating her next question. What was more important, the "why" or the "where from?" In the end, the "why" won. She'd get Emily to search out the "where from" if Levon didn't offer the information.

"Why did your father want to move to Lount's Landing?"

Levon laughed, a harsh, guttural sound. "He gave me some malarkey about facing yesterday so he could save someone tomorrow. I told him I didn't need saving."

"Is that what you argued about?"

"Among other things."

Leave her out of it, Levon had said. "What other things?" she asked.

"He wanted to take the blame for my mother's suicide. I informed him he was twenty-four years too late, that I'd been blaming him since the day she died, and I'd go on blaming him until—"

"Until?"

"Until the day he died."

"Oh."

"Yeah. Oh. Not exactly a conversation I want to relay to Merryfield."

"I think it would be better for you to tell him. If he finds out from someone else, it will look worse for you. He's already caught you in one lie."

"Not telling isn't the same as lying."

And there you have it, Arabella thought. The truth, according to Levon.

12

Apparently murder is good for the newspaper business. *Inside the Landing* had gone from a weekly publication to a daily—at least for the time being—and Arabella had been lucky to get one of the last copies at Cozy Corner Convenience. It was obvious Kerri had no new details, but that didn't stop her from rehashing and sensationalizing what she did know.

The headline, "Shotgun Fired At Start of Golf Tournament," was followed by an explanation of what a shotgun tournament was, along with the information that event organizer Gilly Germaine had fired a real shotgun instead of a starter's pistol. The article went on to say that Levon Larroquette had been acting as the Course Marshal, giving him full access to the course before and during the tournament.

"She's a piece of work," Arabella said, tossing the paper in the blue bin.

"She is that," Emily said. "She's turned a solid small-town newspaper into a tabloid. The upside is she's probably burned Gilly as a source by mentioning the shotgun."

"Small mercies. With friends like Gilly in his corner, Levon doesn't need enemies."

Y

A NEW BLOG entry was posted on *Outside the Landing* less than two hours later, embellishing the few facts Kerri had reported in the paper.

WHERE WAS LEVON LARROQUETTE?
On the day of the Miakoda Falls Golf & Country Club's tournament for Kids Come First, Levon Larroquette, the estranged son of murdered man Marc Larroquette, was acting as Course Marshal. For those readers unfamiliar with the term, a Marshal rides the course to ensure pace of play. Larroquette's EXACT LOCATION on the course at the time of the murder is unknown, as the golfers in the tournament waited in the parking lot by the clubhouse before the tournament's start. However, tournament organizer Gilly Germaine confirmed that Levon had been charged with ensuring all was "in order" on the course before the gun announcing the start of the tournament went off.
The question this blogger has to ask is: Which gun, Gilly? WHICH GUN?

Y

THE NEXT DAY'S newspaper had fresh news: "SON BLAMED MURDERED FATHER FOR MOTHER'S SUICIDE." The report included details of a "private conversation in the park between father and son," as well as a request for anyone with additional information to contact the police.

"Where did Kerri get that information?" Arabella asked Emily as she tried to reach Levon. There

had been no answer on Levon's cell, and despite leaving several messages for him, no return call. Her last attempt had been met with a "voice mailbox full for this user" message.

"Like I said before, she's the queen of rumor and innuendo," Emily said. "Maybe she's just making stuff up. I wouldn't put it past her."

"She isn't making stuff up."

Emily raised her eyebrows. "What haven't you been telling me?"

Arabella filled her in on her last conversation with Levon. It had only been thirty-six hours ago, but it seemed like weeks had passed.

"We know it wasn't you who called Kerri. I wonder who it could have been?"

"Who knows? And really, does it matter? Either way, it looks bad for Levon."

"I have to agree with you there."

"I asked Levon if there were others."

"Others?"

"Marc wanted to make amends with Levon. Maybe there were others he might have wronged?"

"Good point. What did Levon say?"

"That he didn't know." Arabella bit her lip. "I wish I believed him. But he hesitated when I asked.

Only for a fraction of a second, but I heard the pause."

"So what's next?"

"I need you to find out where Marc Larroquette was living before he decided to pull up roots and move here." Arabella caught Emily's look. "I know the police probably know that already, but they're not about to call and tell me, are they?"

"You have a point."

"Maybe knowing where Marc was living will lead us to the mysterious others. And maybe one of the mysterious others will be the one who murdered Marc Larroquette."

"I suppose it's possible," Emily said, though she didn't sound convinced. "Humor me, okay?"

"Consider yourself humored. What about you? What are you going to do?"

"I've got the Pottageville purchases to sort out. If I keep busy enough, I just might stay sane until Levon calls me back." No sooner had she spoken the words than her phone rang. She glanced at the call display. Levon. She answered, her emotions alternating between fear and fury.

"I think the police suspect me of murdering him," Levon said without preamble. Arabella hated the resignation in his voice.

"Kerri's just trying to sell papers and make a name for herself."

"I'm pretty sure this is more serious than her desire to make a name for herself. I've been asked to come into the Miakoda Falls police station to answer a few questions."

"Do you have a lawyer?"

"I have the guy who handled my real estate transactions and wrote my will. I don't think he's equipped to represent a murderer."

"You're not a murderer."

"Let's hope you get selected in my jury trial."

"You identified the body. There's no crime in that."

"I also lied at the scene. Merryfield informs me that lying can be viewed as obstruction of justice. I could go to jail for that while the police build a case against me." Levon's voice cracked. "I hated my father, but I didn't kill him. You have to believe me."

"I believe you," Arabella said. But did she?

Yes, she did. Levon was far from perfect, but he wasn't violent and he wasn't a killer. No matter how hard, or passionately they had fought, there had never been a hint of violence.

"You're being ridiculous. Did Merryfield say you needed a lawyer?"

"No, but he did suggest it might be best to have one present during questioning. I don't know any criminal lawyers. I wondered if you might know one from your days of working at McLelland Insurance."

"The only lawyers we dealt with worked in insurance fraud. It's the wrong specialty."

"Gilly might be able to help."

"Then by all means call her."

"I'm not ready to talk to her. Not yet. Not after what she told Kerri St. Amour."

"If it helps, I'll call her for you."

"Thank you."

Arabella went through her contacts as soon as Levon hung up.

She found the entry for Gilly Germaine and dialed. One ring, two rings, three—

"Arabella?"

"Levon asked me to call you."

"Why wouldn't he just call me himself?" Her tone was a mix between cross and curious, snooty and sincere.

Because Levon doesn't trust you, Gilly, and probably for good reason. Because in spite of their past—or maybe because of it—Arabella and Levon were always going to be one another's first call, whether Gilly wanted to acknowledge it or not.

Maybe that's what Aaron meant when he'd told her he couldn't be number two if there was no chance of becoming number one.

"The police want to question Levon about the murder of his father."

"We were all questioned in the clubhouse."

"He's been asked to go to the Miakoda Falls Police Station for more formal questioning. He thought with your connections you might be able to recommend a good criminal defense lawyer."

There was a long silence. "Yet he called you instead of me."

"There were other things to discuss."

"I see." Her tone positively icy now.

Arabella was losing patience. "Do you know someone, or not? Because if you don't, I have other calls to make."

"Let me get back to you with an answer one way or another. I promise to do so within the next two hours."

"I'll be waiting."

Y

THE PHONE RANG again just as Emily wandered into the shop. Arabella gave a quick wave of acknowledgment before answering.

"What do you have for me?"

Emily tilted her head, raised her eyebrows, and gave Arabella a "who is it" look.

Arabella ignored her.

"The name of the lawyer is Isla Kempenfelt," Gilly said. "She comes highly recommended. She's young, ambitious, and willing to do whatever it takes to win. Even better, she's willing to take on Levon's case pro bono, should he actually get charged with anything. She's expecting your call."

Arabella was already Googling Isla Kempenfelt on her tablet. A photo showed a fine-boned woman with delicate features, wheat-blonde hair, and eyes the color of milk chocolate. Her office was in Marketville, the largest town in Cedar County, located thirty minutes south of Lount's Landing.

"Thank you, Gilly. Levon will be most appreciative."

Gilly laughed, a dry, humorless sound. "Give him my regards, Arabella. He's all yours now, if indeed there was ever a time he wasn't. A woman in my position can't afford to date a man who's suspected of murder."

"Surely you don't believe he's guilty?"

"It doesn't matter what I think, Arabella. Or what you think, for that matter. Perception is everything. I'm afraid the charities I work with wouldn't want that sort of stigma attached to me, and I do have to earn a living. I thought Kerri wanted details about organizing the golf tournament and she practically implicated me with the insinuation about the shotgun——" Gilly caught herself and changed the subject. "Besides, it's not like Levon and I were serious, not really. We were just having fun."

Arabella stared at the phone for a long time after Gilly hung up. She doubted that Gilly Germaine had ever done anything "just for fun" in her entire life. She suspected that Gilly had been talking to Kerri about more than the golf tournament or Levon being Course Marshal. Not that she'd ever be able to prove anything. She walked over to Emily, who had been sitting at her computer, pretending to be busy.

"Gilly just dumped Levon over the phone."

"How did he take it?" Emily asked.

"I haven't told him yet."

13

ARABELLA UPDATED EMILY with a quick recap of the morning's events, including the phone call with Gilly.

"I've heard of Isla Kempenfelt," Emily said. "She's developing quite a reputation as a criminal defense attorney. Gilly must have called in a few favors to get her to defend Levon pro bono."

"She has experience with first-degree murder trials?"

"Hmm…actually, no. She's done more along the lines of vehicular manslaughter. Remember the case a few months back? A woman was coming back from her bachelorette party and went through a stop sign, t-boned a car coming the other way. The driver and the passenger of the other vehicle were killed, the bride-to-be escaped with barely a scratch. It was a loser of a case if there ever was one, but Kempenfelt managed to get her client a sentence of five years in jail plus probation."

Arabella remembered the case—it had been radio talk show fodder for months—she just hadn't connected it to Kempenfelt. For the prosecution, the crown attorney had been going for a ten-year sentence, and most folks figured the bride-to-be would get at least eight.

Nevertheless, vehicular manslaughter was a far cry from being accused of murdering your own father, though the sad fact remained that Levon didn't have the resources to pay what were bound to be hefty legal fees in this case. She just hoped this Isla Kempenfelt was as good as Gilly and Emily seemed to think she was.

Y

ISLA KEMPENFELT STOPPED by the Glass Dolphin on her way to the Miakoda Falls police station. The impression Arabella had from the online photos of a fine-boned woman with delicate features was quickly quashed. This woman might have been fine-boned, but she was as tough as Teflon and likely just as slick.

"I've called Detective Merryfield and told him I'm on my way," Kempenfelt said. "They won't question Levon without me present. However, I wanted to talk to you first. What can you tell me about his relationship with Marc Larroquette?"

For the first time, Arabella realized she only had Levon's version of his father's story. Until now, she'd always taken him at his word. Could she trust his word? She'd trusted him on other matters only to find out he had lied or withheld large portions of the truth. Why should the story he told her about his father be any different?

"Only what he's told me. He grew up in Scarborough in a 1950s bungalow on what he called the wrong side of Highway 401. One day, his father went out for cigarettes and never came back." Arabella blushed. It was the sort of story you heard about on television and movies. Did it ever actually happen like that? If Kempenfelt had the same train of thought, she didn't vocalize it. "Okay. Daddy goes out for a pack of smokes, mom and Levon are left behind. What happens next?"

"Mrs. Larroquette…" Arabella suddenly realized she didn't even know Levon's mother's first name, a sad reflection on their relationship when you thought about it. "His mother started drinking, taking prescription meds, and couldn't hold down a job. One day she closed the garage door, sat inside her car, and left it running. By the time they found her, she was dead from carbon monoxide poisoning."

"How old was Levon?"

"Seventeen. He was lucky, if you could call it that. At the time his mother was trying to kill herself, he was attempting to steal something from the local convenience store. The cop who got the call took pity on Levon and managed to get him into a boot camp for young offenders in Miakoda Falls. He's been on the straight and narrow ever since."

Kempenfelt was writing furiously on a yellow legal pad. She looked up when she was finished, a frown furrowing her brow.

"I'm going to need a few more details about his father."

"You'll have to get them from Levon. He doesn't talk about his past. I'm surprised that I know as much as I do."

"What about the day of the tournament? Did you see Levon before finding the body?"

Arabella nodded and filled Kempenfelt in: they were there setting up their silent auction items; he wasn't agitated; nothing seemed unusual.

"How much time passed between when you spoke to him in the silent auction room until you saw him at the third hole?"

"About thirty minutes, give or take. The golfers were asked to wait by their golf carts in the parking lot."

Kempenfelt didn't have to say it. Fifteen minutes was more than enough time to kill someone, drive away in a golf cart to another part of the course, and come back after the body was discovered.

"Don't worry, Arabella," Kempenfelt said, as if reading her mind. "I've got this. You just have to go back to living your life." She hesitated a moment, then said. "You do have a local reputation for 'inquiring.' Gilly Germaine implied that you get involved in matters that don't concern you. Whether that's the case or not, I want Levon to be focused and clear, not wondering what his ex-wife, Gilly, or anyone else is up to."

Arabella bit back a retort and nodded, though she had no intention of acquiescing to Isla Kempenfelt—let alone Gilly Germaine. The first thing she was going to do when she got back was convince Emily to help her clear Levon of this charge. If it cost them customers or turned them into the pariahs of Main Street, that was just the price you had to pay for family. Because divorced or not, Levon was still her family. Always was, always would be.

She hoped he'd been telling her the truth about his past, that he hadn't left out something important. A detail, however small, that would come back to incriminate him.

Even as the thought crossed her mind, she knew in her gut that he had. Levon never sweated the fine print.

14

ARABELLA ARRIVED at the Glass Dolphin just before closing time. She was alternately pleased and annoyed to find Emily photographing a collection of knitting sheaths and clew-baskets.

Arabella had picked them up at auction for a song, and while Emily would need her help on the details, it was good to know she was taking the initiative to update items for sale on eBay and the website's inventory. At least one of them had their eye on making enough money to pay the rent. Food—something outside of tinned tuna, peanut butter, and pasta—would be a bonus. So she should have been happy. But a big part of her wondered why Emily wasn't pacing, waiting to hear about her meeting with Isla Kempenfelt.

Emily put the camera down. "Finally. I was going stir crazy here. Fill me in."

Arabella breathed a sigh of relief. Emily cared. Right now she needed the friendship more than the partnership. She was about to update her on the latest in the Levon saga when Luke Surmanski and Hudson Tanaka strolled into the Glass Dolphin.

"We thought we'd update you on the hole in one insurance," Luke said. "Apparently, since the tournament officially started, we're out of luck getting any sort of refund."

"Well, that sucks," Emily said, "but you didn't have to come all the way here. You could have called."

"We could have," Luke admitted, "but after reading Kerri's articles and that blog…I don't know what we can do to help but—"

Hudson interrupted. "It can't be easy for either of you."

"Is there any other reason for your visit?" As soon as she said it, Arabella knew that it sounded snarky. Emily's quick glance in her direction confirmed it. But she wanted to tell Emily about her plan to clear Levon and she wanted to tell her now.

If either Luke or Hudson was offended, they didn't show it. Nor did they offer to leave. Instead, their words tumbled onto one another's as they said they wanted to find out the truth and to help in any way they could.

"Not that I'm ungrateful," Arabella said, "but we've only known each other a couple of months and you don't know Levon at all. So I guess I'm asking, why? What's in it for you?"

"Arabella," Emily said, her face flushed scarlet. "There's no need to be rude. Maybe Luke and Hudson feel connected to this because they were there when you found the body?"

Arabella was embarrassed. "I'm sorry, Luke, Hudson. This whole affair has gotten the better of my manners."

"No apologies necessary," Hudson said. "Emily is right. We do feel connected, and concerned.

But there's more, right Luke?"

Luke looked down at his feet and did a bit of a shuffle before looking up. "The thing is, the body did look familiar, but I couldn't place him, at least not there and then. I didn't want to say anything until I was sure."

"And now you're sure?" Emily asked.

Luke nodded. "He was wearing a baseball cap and sunglasses, but I'm sure he's the same man who rented a houseboat from the marina about a week ago. Except his ID didn't say Marc Larroquette. If it had, I would have connected him to Levon, or at least asked him if there was a family connection."

"What name did he go by?" Arabella asked. "Kevin Hollister Cartwright."

"That doesn't make any sense," Emily said. "Are you sure that was the name the man used?" Luke nodded. "Positive. Why?"

"Because Kevin Hollister Cartwright is my ex-fiancé. And the last time I checked, he was thirty- five, living in Toronto, and very much alive."

15

ARABELLA GOT OUT THE SHORTBREAD. If there was ever a time for cookie therapy, this was it. She opened the tin and offered it around. There were no takers. Fine, more cookies for me. "Did you tell the police about the houseboat rental, Luke?"

Luke shook his head. "Not yet, although of course I have to, and I will as soon as I leave here. In truth, I should have gone there first, but I didn't want you to be blindsided. I also thought you might have something to add." He gave Emily an appraising look. "It seems you did, though I'll admit I wasn't expecting it to be an introduction to your ex-fiancé."

"You can't think that I had anything to do with this?" Emily said. "I moved here from Toronto eight months ago. I didn't know Levon or Arabella before that, and I certainly didn't know Marc Larroquette."

"Then why would he use your ex-fiancé's name?"

"You tell me and we'll both know, but there has to be a reason. Maybe he's just messing with the people in Arabella's life."

"Maybe," Arabella said, but she wasn't convinced. A thought crossed her mind. "What sort of ID did Marc Larroquette have?"

"A Pleasure Craft Operating card."

"Do you need that to rent a houseboat?"

"Not in Ontario, but that's what he used as ID. He told me that he was simplifying his life and no longer used credit cards. He paid cash for a one month rental, plus a five-hundred-dollar damage deposit." Luke grimaced. "In hindsight, maybe I should have been suspicious, but I've had people pay cash before, and it's never been a problem. It's the same paperwork for cash or credit when I do my taxes."

"What about the Pleasure Craft Operator card?" Emily asked. "The one that had Kevin's name on it?"

"It's easy to get a boat license in Canada. There's a three-hour class or you can do a five-chapter course on the website for fifty dollars. Anyone can take the test online, and as long as they manage to get seventy-five percent, they get a license for life. They can even retake the course as many times as necessary until they pass. But here's the kicker—there's no photo on the boating license."

"So he could have taken the test as Kevin Hollister Cartwright and no one would have been the wiser," Emily said.

"Exactly," Luke said. "Which brings us back to where we started."

Maybe not quite where they'd started, Arabella thought. At least they had another name, albeit one that was Emily's ex. It was a thin lead, that much was true, but it was something. Now all she had to do was convince Emily to call her ex-fiancé.

"I don't want to do it," Emily said for the umpteenth time. She was back at the computer, uploading the knitting sheath and clew-basket photographs, a magazine open on the desk. "Besides, I'm busy trying to make us some much-needed money. There was a great article on them by Lucinda Seward in the March 2016 issue of New England Antiques Journal. Did you know that eighteenth- and nineteenth-century knitters were multitaskers?" Emily picked up the magazine and began reading.

"In order to keep one hand free to rock a baby, carry kindling, beat an egg—anything that involved one hand only, they pinned one of these devices to a garment or fitted it to a belt, and then used it to hold one of the knitting needles while continuing to knit with the other. Knitting sheaths were often used alongside yarn holders that were also attached to the woman's clothes or belts. These bags or baskets were called 'clew-baskets,'—that's spelled C-L-E-W—which is an old word for a ball of thread. Her belt might also hold a hook to hold up larger pieces of knitting and save them from dragging. It all puts a new twist on the idea of work clothes."

A big part of Arabella was impressed. Emily was really trying to learn the antiques trade, and she did a lot of research. New England Antiques Journal had become one of her favorite resources. Normally, Arabella would have been happy to see Emily's enthusiasm. It was true they needed the money, except that right now Levon was being questioned for a murder he didn't commit, and she needed Emily to focus on the investigation. Still, she had to play this one right if she wanted Emily's help. And she did want it. Emily had been a journalist for years. She knew how to investigate and interview—a skill set that Arabella didn't possess. "I did know that, but I would never have put it into that context, as if these women were the original multitaskers. What a great comparison. Good on you for finding that article."

"Thank you. I'm having a lot of fun researching and learning."

Arabella took a deep breath. "I really do appreciate all that you're doing for the Glass Dolphin.

It's just that—"

"I know. It's just that you're worried about Levon." Emily sighed. "There's something I haven't told you. I heard from an old friend in Toronto last week—and I use the term 'friend' loosely. She told me that Kevin and Chloe are getting married in October. It's bad enough that he dumped me for that platinum blonde bimbo who calls herself a personal trainer, but to marry her…honestly, I thought I was over him, what with dating Luke and all, but it still stings. That was supposed to be us getting married."

"I'm sorry. You know I wouldn't ask if I didn't think it was important."

"I know, and you're right. My discomfort is nothing compared to what Levon must be going through right now. I'll call Kevin. But if he gloats about Chloe, we just might have another murder on our hands."

Emily arranged to meet Kevin at the Starbucks in Toronto's Union Station. "Not that I want to drink coffee with that man," she'd told Arabella, "but I'd rather ask him about Marc Larroquette in person. Kevin is a consummate liar, but if he knows anything at all, I'll get it out of him."

With Emily away, Arabella had no option but to stay in the shop, not that she expected any customers. It was midweek in July, the height of vacation season, and while the Lakeside merchants enjoyed their fair share of summer visitors, Lount's Landing was a good thirty-minute drive away. Historic Main Street, despite the efforts of local business, was not enough of a destination to draw them in. Even the once vibrant Main Street Merchants' Association had started to fizzle out; everyone wanted to be the boss but no one wanted to do the work. In retrospect, maybe Emily's jet ski promotion idea hadn't been so bad.

She had just started unpacking the last box from the Pottageville auction—a nice assortment of Cornflower glassware that was always a good seller, especially the salt-and-pepper shakers and cream-and-sugar sets—when the bell on the door tinkled to announce a customer. Arabella glanced up, surprised to find five people entering the store. Before long, the shop was filled with folks milling around, picking up things and setting them down, followed by the inevitable question of "what's the best you can do on this such-and-such?" Arabella was more than happy to negotiate, but she still had to turn a profit. Fortunately, most people were reasonable, and if they weren't, Arabella's acerbic response either got them there or out the door.

Customer traffic stayed steady throughout the day, and Arabella found herself too busy to think about Emily, for which she was grateful. By the time six o'clock rolled around, she'd run up several hundred dollars in sales. Her best sale was to a man by the name of Windsor Scott, who bought three oak end tables in assorted sizes and a child's rocking chair, paying sticker price for the lot, and promising to come back soon. It was by far the most successful day she'd had since her open house eight months earlier.

It wasn't until a few minutes before closing time, when a woman asked, "Did Levon help you pick that lovely vase?" that Arabella finally connected the dots: being the ex-wife of a suspected murderer, it seemed, was good for business.

Emily got off the GO train at Union Station and wound her way through the maze of commuters. Since moving to Lount's Landing, she seldom came back to the city—too many memories, most of them bad—but when she did, she preferred transit to driving. The Don Valley Parkway, the main north-south artery into downtown Toronto, had long ago earned the nickname the "Don Valley Parking Lot." She shook her head at the construction going on around Union. It had been ongoing for as long as she could remember, with every campaigning politician over the past decade promising to do something about it and Toronto's ever-increasing gridlock. Maybe if Toronto's city council stopped arguing about subways versus light rail and actually put a shovel to the ground, they'd get folks moving again.

The Starbucks was packed as usual, although at this time of the morning most people grabbed their drinks to go. Emily spotted Kevin in the lineup and wondered whether to join him or politely take her place at the back of the queue. Her inner debate came to an end when Kevin called out that he'd get her nonfat, no foam latte. She wanted to tell him that she was off that kick since moving to Lount's Landing, which didn't have a Starbucks and probably never would. These days she preferred regular coffee, black, one sugar, but she didn't want to cause a scene.

Emily grabbed the first available seats and studied Kevin. He looked good, better than good. Buff, to be honest. His sandy hair was shorter than it used to be, almost military short, but it suited his square jaw. Mostly he looked happy. Happier than when he'd been with her, at least in the last few months when all they'd done was argue about everything from the kind of pasta to buy—white penne or whole wheat rigatoni—to what movie to see on Saturday night.

Kevin liked Woody Allen films, which he considered brilliant. Emily couldn't get beyond Allen's personal life and refused to support him, brilliant or not.

Kevin slid into the seat opposite her and handed her the latte. She didn't offer to pay him for it, knowing it would only set him off. If Kevin bought you something, you didn't argue. You accepted it, even if you didn't necessarily want what he was offering. She took the lid off, took a sip, and murmured a quiet thanks.

"No problem, though I'll admit you've piqued my curiosity. What's so important that you made the trek into the city? That we couldn't talk about it on the phone?"

Thoughts began running across Emily's mind like a ticker-tape marquee. No "you're looking good, how's it going" type of pleasantries. Just straight down to business. Well, what did she expect, a dozen red roses and a box of chocolates?

"I was playing in a charity golf tournament two days ago. Our group discovered a man on the third hole—a dead man. He'd been shot."

"Wow. That must have been traumatic."

Why was it that he looked more impressed than surprised?

"You could say that. He'd been renting a houseboat from Luke's Marina in Lakeside, which isn't unusual in the summer."

"And you know this how?"

"Luke is a friend of mine." Emily blushed at Kevin's knowing grin. "Anyway, that's not the point.

The point is, he rented it using your name."

"My name?"

Emily nodded. "Your full name. Kevin Hollister Cartwright. He used a Pleasure Craft Operator's license. Boat licenses don't have photo IDs on them, but because he paid cash up front, Luke considered it sufficient."

"Luke sounds like a very trusting individual." He said in a tone that implied Luke was also an idiot.

"What can I say? Small town values." Emily pulled the page from *Inside the Landing* out of her purse and passed it over to Kevin, pointing to the police artist's sketch. "This is the man. Do you know him?"

The color drained from Kevin's face. "He's Chloe's stepfather. Marc Laurentian. But what was he doing in Lount's Landing, and why did he use my name?"

16

Emily stared at Kevin. Could it be possible? Was Chloe really related to Levon? "Marc was Chloe's stepfather?"

"Yes. He married her mom ten years ago. Chloe was twelve."

Which made Chloe twenty-two now, ten years younger than her, and thirteen years younger than Kevin. Focus on the task at hand, Emily. At least she's not Levon's sister.

"What was Chloe's mother's name?"

"Alice."

"Did she change her last name?"

"I never asked, but Chloe's last name is Brampton. Why?"

"I'm trying to get all the facts."

"Once a reporter, always a reporter," Kevin said, but he said it with a smile.

"You said his name was Marc Laurentian. The police identified him as Marc Larroquette."

A couple next to them had stopped talking and started listening. Kevin must have noticed too, because he suggested taking a walk on the PATH. The PATH was downtown Toronto's multi- directional underground walkway, linking nineteen miles of retail space. Emily got lost whenever she tried to navigate it.

"Sure, as long as you promise to get me back to Union Station."

"Some things never change," Kevin said, but his tone was affectionate.

They walked along without talking for the first five minutes, both of them lost in their thoughts. It felt almost like the old days, before the fights and the drama that had taken over their lives. The moment was spoiled when they walked past the gym that Kevin had belonged to and where Chloe worked as a personal trainer. It hadn't taken long for Chloe's training to become very personal. The next thing Emily knew, Kevin gave her a Cooking For One cookbook and announced they were done.

"As I was saying, his real name is Marc Larroquette." She knew her voice sounded strained and wanted to kick herself.

Get over it, Emily.

If Kevin noticed, he ignored it. "He must have changed his last name to Laurentian. Maybe he had a good reason."

"What sort of good reason?"

"I don't know. Maybe he went bankrupt or something and wanted a fresh start." He wanted a fresh start, all right—one that didn't involve his old family. "Was Chloe close to him?"

"Not at all. Alice died in a car accident when Chloe was eighteen, and from what I can gather, Marc wasn't the paternal type. Chloe left Goulais right after high school and moved to Toronto. She's never gone back."

"Who's 'Gooley'?"

"It's not a who, it's a where. The Goulais River, G-O-U-L-A-I-S. It's about forty-five minutes northwest of Sault Ste. Marie, on Lake Superior. Beautiful country. I camped up in Pancake Bay Provincial Park when I was in university. It's about as far from urban living as you can get. Chloe might have been born there, but she's definitely a city girl."

Emily figured stilettos, skintight clothes, and spray-on tans wouldn't be the fashion of choice in a place like Goulais. "Did she stay in touch with Marc?"

"She didn't talk much about Marc. I gathered she hadn't seen him for years. Then he called her ten days ago, said he was in

Toronto for a meeting, and asked if he could see her. She agreed to meet him for coffee." Kevin frowned. "I offered to go with her, but she insisted on meeting him alone."

"Do you know what he wanted?"

"Apparently he was trying to make amends with everyone he'd hurt in his life, starting with the most recent offenses."

"Sounds like Alcoholics Anonymous. I think they have a step like that."

"Except that wasn't it. Marc had joined an association, although to my mind it sounded more like a cult. The group was called FYSST. They're based out of Thornbury."

Thornbury was a four-season resort community about two hours northwest of Toronto. It was known for good skiing, apples, and the waters of Georgian Bay. It wasn't the sort of place you'd expect a cult to start up.

"Fist? As in punch someone with your fist?"

"No, as in F-Y-S-S-T, an anagram. It stands for Face Yesterday, Save Someone Tomorrow."

What was it Levon had said to Arabella? Something about Marc telling him he was there to face yesterday. Emily tried to keep her expression neutral. She could just imagine Kevin's reaction when Chloe told him about FYSST. He was never much on organized religion. Something like FYSST would set his inner radar on high alert.

"Where did Marc fit in?"

"He told Chloe that he was in charge of the Northern Ontario chapter. She didn't ask if he'd recruited any members." Kevin stopped walking and led them to a bench. He turned toward her, his brown eyes serious. "I would never say this to Chloe, but my guess is that Marc Laurentian was nothing more than a con man."

If it was a con, it was his last, Emily thought. "What if someone wanted to join FYSST? Is there a cost to do that? Some sort of initiation fee or donation to the cause?"

Kevin shook his head. "I don't know. Chloe said he didn't ask her for money, but even if he did, she might not have told me."

Translation: they'd been fighting about money.

Emily predicted a cookbook for one in Chloe's future. She almost felt sorry for her. "Did Chloe forgive him?"

"She did. She said he'd done the best he could. She admitted that she hadn't made life easy for him, either. I gather she would have preferred her mother remain single. According to Chloe, they promised to get together again the next time Marc was in the city. We thought he'd gone back to Goulais River. Now you tell me that he was in Lakeside, renting a houseboat under my name."

"And found dead at the Miakoda Falls Golf and Country Club," Emily said dryly. She chewed the inside of her lip, thinking. The short odds were that Marc Larroquette, aka Marc Laurentian, had gone to Lakeside with the intention of seeing Levon and asking for forgiveness under the guise of FYSST.

According to the latest post on *Outside the Landing*, the "prominent local realtor" alleged there had been "others" involved in Marc's efforts at reconciliation. It appeared that Chloe had been one of the others. She needed to tell Arabella what she'd just learned.

"I've got to get back to Lount's Landing. Can you point me in the direction of Union Station?" Kevin stood up. "I'll do you one better. I'll walk you there."

They were within spitting distance of Union Station when Emily noticed Chloe strutting toward them, chest thrust out, hands on hips, her black spandex tights and leopard-print top accentuating every curve. How long had she been following them? Since they'd passed her gym the first time? Or on the way back? Emily didn't know and was relieved to find out that she didn't care.

Unless, of course, Chloe knew more about Marc Larroquette than she had shared with Kevin.

Damn it. She'd have talk to Chloe.

But not today. Today, Chloe was Kevin's problem. Emily patted Kevin's arm, letting her hand linger slightly longer than necessary, then gave him a peck on the cheek.

She wound her way through the throng of commuters to Platform 26, humming *Bad Timing* by Blue Rodeo. It was time to go home.

17

ARABELLA PACED THE SHOP FLOOR, nibbling on a shortbread cookie as Emily filled her in on her conversation with Kevin. She was going to give them up…once she emptied the tin.

"You're telling me that Marc Larroquette was living in Goulais River for the past ten years as Marc Laurentian."

"At least ten years," Emily said. "That's when he married Chloe's mother, Alice. It's possible he's been there longer than that."

"I need to speak to Levon about this. I wonder if he knows Chloe? What's her last name?"

"Brampton. Kevin wasn't sure whether or not her mother changed her name to Laurentian."

"The easiest way to find out is to talk to Chloe."

"It's not as easy as you think. I don't want to talk to her, and I can pretty much guarantee she feels the same way. Especially since…"

"Since what? What did you do?"

"Chloe was following us on the PATH. I gave Kevin a peck on the cheek. I might have let my hand rest on his arm a bit longer than was absolutely necessary before entering the GO train station."

"Classy."

"Admittedly not my finest hour, but I might have done her a favor. I think Kevin is getting ready to dump her. He intimated they'd been arguing about money, and he didn't seem too pleased to see her on the PATH. Either way, I think it's probably best if I wait a while before calling her."

"Maybe Kevin will break up with her and Chloe will call you—" Arabella blushed. "Did I just say that out loud?"

"Yeah. You did. Let's just say I won't be waiting by the phone. In the meantime, it's time to go to Plan B."

"What's Plan B?"

"I don't know. But we'll figure something out."

PLAN B TURNED out to be a visit to Levon's farmhouse on the outskirts of town. He'd called Arabella. He kept details sparse, but he wanted her to know that he was back from the police station and he asked her to come to his house.

His tone of voice indicated he needed her help. She wondered if he was going to tell her the whole truth or hold back information. After their divorce, they'd gradually gone from barely making peace with one another to becoming friends again, but she'd never been to his new home until today.

The exterior was slate blue board-and-batten with carefully painted cream trim. Pink and purple verbena cascaded out of window boxes. Two vintage wicker rockers and a round wicker side table stood on the front porch. Arabella remembered being with Levon the day he bought them. She fought the lump forming in her throat, pushing the thought aside and focusing on how much Emily would love this Victorian house. It was on about an acre of land, with a stream running along the west side of the property, and a row of trees acting as a natural fence along the east. A large wooden barn, painted rustic red, would be where Levon kept his antique finds and where he'd restore and refinish the furniture when warranted.

"Sometimes you have to leave the age in, and sometimes,"

Levon had told her, his words befitting a person with years of experience and a practiced eye, "the only way to sell a piece is to make it pretty again."

She was still taking it all in when Levon sauntered out onto the porch. He looked every bit his forty years plus a few, the dark circles under his indigo eyes emphasizing an unusually pale complexion. Even his trademark shaggy brown hair looked limp and tired.

"How are you holding up?"

"How do you think?"

"I can leave if I'm bothering you."

Levon grimaced. "You're right, you didn't deserve that. Have a seat on the porch. Can I get you something? Coffee? Tea? Something stronger?"

"A glass of wine would be nice. Chardonnay if you have it."

"I do."

"Just a small one, though. I'm driving."

"You can always stay over."

"That's probably not a great idea."

"I meant in the spare bedroom."

Arabella blushed. "Yeah, I knew that."

Levon grinned. "Sure you did. Let me get the drinks."

They settled into the wicker chairs, Levon with a Sleeman's Honey Brown Lager and Arabella with an Australian Chardonnay. For a few minutes, they rocked in companionable silence. Neither one wanted to ruin the mood, even though they both knew the mood would have to be ruined.

Levon went first.

"Thanks for arranging the lawyer. Isla Kempenfelt was very impressive."

"You can thank Gilly for that."

"Hmm. Funny, she's not answering my calls."

"It seems that your potential incarceration for murder is bad for her reputation."

A flicker of hurt, then, "I guess I shouldn't be surprised. Appearances are important to Gilly."

"Too important, if you ask me."

"Claws in, Bella, and let's face facts. Gilly dumping me is the least of my problems." She had to admit he was right. "What happened at the police station?"

"Merryfield left me alone in the interview room until Isla Kempenfelt arrived. You'd think that would have calmed my nerves, but it only served to agitate me more. The room wasn't much bigger than a broom closet where I waited and wondered...you can't imagine what that felt like."

Arabella knew what it was like to be left waiting and wondering and hadn't liked it, though she had to admit that the circumstances had been nowhere near as dire. "What happened when Kempenfelt got there?"

"Merryfield let her come into the interview room and speak to me first. We talked about the possibility of my being charged with obstruction of justice. Isla—"

"Isla? You're already on a first-name basis with your lawyer?"

Levon sighed. "Why the hell does that matter? And yes, to answer your question, she suggested it as soon as we met. She said it would make it easier for me to confide in her."

"You're right, it doesn't matter. Did *Isla* think you could be charged with obstruction of justice?"

"She didn't think the police would take that route, and she was correct."

"That's good news."

"Is it? She does believe they're trying to build a case against me. Her strategy was to determine what they knew by the questions Merryfield asked. She did say there was one big thing in my favor."

"What was that?"

"There's no direct evidence against me."

"Meaning?"

"No one saw me shoot Marc Larroquette."

18

LEVON ROCKED BACK and forth as if he didn't have a care in the world. "Relax, Arabella," he said, "I didn't shoot my father, which means that since I wasn't there at the time he was shot, no one could have seen me do it."

Arabella expelled a long breath. "You had me worried there for a minute."

"Thanks for the vote of confidence. I thought you believed in me."

"I do. It's just that you lied, and not just to the police. You lied to all of us at the golf course. Me.

Emily. Luke. Hudson. Trent Norland."

"Trent Norland?"

"The guy from the insurance company."

"Oh yeah. The guy with the baseball cap and the plaid pants."

"That's the one. You lied to all of us."

Levon stopped rocking and leaned forward. "Oh. My. God. You're the one who told the police that I met with my father. But how on earth did you find out?"

Arabella drained the rest of her wine and handed the empty glass to Levon. "Not necessarily, but it looks like I'll be staying overnight after all. Better make up the spare bed and then pour me another glass, please. We've got lots to talk about."

Y

LEVON CAME BACK to the porch about ten minutes later, and told Arabella that he put a pair of old flannel pajama pants and a tee shirt on the bed for her to sleep in. "They'll be a bit big on you," he said, "but the pants have a drawstring and the tee shirt won't matter."

They sat down and as if by unspoken agreement, he started by talking about his interview at the Miakoda Falls Police Station with Merryfield and Aaron Beecham. "Merryfield started by telling me that they would be videotaping the interview. Kempenfelt had already told me that was standard operating procedure—to protect both sides, she said—so it didn't come as a surprise, but it still felt invasive, more like an interrogation, you know?"

Arabella nodded. She didn't know, but she could imagine.

"Once all that was set up, Merryfield walked us through the five main facts thus far." Levon lifted his hand and started counting on his fingers. "One. My father walked out on my mom and me twenty- four years ago. Two. The man they found dead on the golf course, Marc Larroquette, was my father and a victim of foul play. Three. I told the police that I hadn't seen Marc Larroquette for those twenty- four years. Four. Someone had reported seeing me with Marc Larroquette in the park a couple of days before. Five. That we had been arguing."

"I didn't tell Aaron that you'd been arguing."

"But he surmised it, from what you did or didn't say."

"Yes. I'm so sorry."

Levon shook his head. "It's not your fault. You had to tell the truth. If I'd done that in the first place, I might be in a much better position than I am now. Besides, it's a small town. It's hard to hide anything. I should have remembered that. Merryfield said that between Kerri St. Amour's 'reporting' and that blog a half dozen people have come forward to say they saw me in the park that day.

I'm assuming they all confirmed your statement. Beecham chimed in and asked what we'd been arguing about. There was a bit of jockeying back and forth between him and Kempenfelt, but she eventually agreed to let me answer the question."

"What did you tell them?"

"I told them what happened."

"What did happen?"

Levon took a long swallow of his second beer and began rocking again. "He—I won't dignify the man by calling him my father—called me about a week ago. He said he was in the area and needed to see me. I hung up on him."

"Let me guess. He kept calling."

"Bingo. I finally agreed to meet with him at the park. I had no idea what he wanted, but I figured if we met in a public place, he wouldn't try anything funny. We met by the water fountain and he tried to hug me when I got there. I wasn't having any of it. That man broke my mother in a hundred pieces. What kind of man walks out on his family and never comes back?"

Arabella didn't have an answer for that. Her own parents had been overprotective clinging vines, strict to the point of strangulation. In her mind, one type of parent wasn't any better than the other. "Why did he come back?"

"I told you before that he wanted to make amends for leaving, for my mom's suicide, but it went deeper than that. He was involved with an association called fist, spelled F-Y-S-S-T. It stands for—"

"Face Yesterday, Save Someone Tomorrow."

"How did you know?"

"That's one of the things I wanted to talk to you about. But I shouldn't have interrupted you."

"Marc seemed to think that all he had to do was come back and all would be forgiven. As if that's all it took. But I've told you all this before. All except for the FYSST part, but apparently you already know about that."

"Did you tell the police everything?"

Levon stared at his hands. "Pretty much word for word what I've told you. I admitted knowing he planned to move here and was looking at houses with Poppy. I told them the part about saying that I wouldn't forgive him until the day he died."

"Did you say anything else?"

"Not to the police and not to Isla Kempenfelt." Still staring at his hands.

Arabella resisted the urge to scream. "What about to Marc Larroquette? Did you say anything else to him?"

Levon finally looked up, his face a study in abject misery. "I told him not only that I wouldn't forgive him, but he was as good as dead to me. It wasn't a threat, Arabella. It was a statement. I just don't know if the police will see it that way.

19

ARABELLA TOOK another sip of wine. Saying someone was dead to you wasn't a threat, but could it be construed as one? She had to believe it might, especially when combined with Levon's original lie to the police. But did that make it right to withhold the statement? "You should have told Kempenfelt," Arabella said. "She could have advised you. It's not too late to do that."

Levon shook his head. "We left it that she'd be there for me, should I find myself in need of a lawyer. At this point, according to Merryfield, I'm free to go about my business." He let out a dry chuckle. "As long as my business doesn't take me out of Cedar County—which makes it tough to earn a living as an antiques picker. People aren't about to bring the contents of their house to me."

"What about Shuggie?" Shuggie St. Pierre had been Levon's apprentice for the past fourteen months.

"Shuggie is a hard worker, and he's learned a lot in a relatively short amount of time, but he still has a lot to learn. A month ago, he bought a group of mason jars and insulators from someone who claimed to be a longtime collector. Lovely amber, emerald, and amethyst colors, but—"

"Totally fake." Arabella knew there were plenty of unscrupulous sellers who wouldn't balk at the obvious. Someone had altered the composition of clear glass using any number of techniques, all readily available online. While most of the articles were aimed at the do-it-yourselfer who simply wanted to create a vintage look, there were always those willing to take advantage of an unsuspecting buyer like Shuggie.

"Let me go with Shuggie if something comes up outside of Cedar County. Now that Emily is at the shop, I have a bit more latitude." She caught Levon's look. "Hey, this isn't charity. Fair's fair. If Shuggie spots something first, and it's legit, it's his and yours. If I spot it first, it's mine. If there's enough for both of us, no matter who finds what first, we split it fifty-fifty."

"I can live with that."

Arabella smiled. "You're welcome. Now it's my turn. Pour me another glass of wine and let me tell you what I know."

Y

ARABELLA STARTED AT THE BEGINNING, with Luke's visit to the Glass Dolphin. She omitted the part about Hudson being there too, not that she had any rational reason for doing so.

"Luke said he recognized your father as a man who had rented a houseboat from him about a week ago. He paid cash up front for a month, plus a damage deposit, using a Pleasure Craft Operator's card as ID."

"So that's where he was staying. I wondered about that." Levon frowned. "It's funny. He was apparently looking for a house, but I had the distinct impression he wasn't looking for a long reunion. If anything, the whole FYYST business seemed like a scam to me—a way to make money."

Arabella nodded. According to Emily, Kevin had suspected much the same thing. She asked Levon, "Did he ask you for money?"

"No, but I never gave him the chance."

"Who else do you suppose he was here to see?" Finding out

could be a lead to the murderer. Arabella's pulse quickened, anticipating the thought of passing the info to Emily.

It was as if Levon read her mind. "I have no idea, but before you get the lame-brained idea to find out, stop. It's too dangerous, and I don't want you to get involved."

"I'm already involved. And Emily, too."

"Emily? Why?"

Arabella hedged, not quite ready to tell Levon everything at once. "Emily was a journalist for years, remember?"

"Writing about the housing market and looking for a murderer are two very different things."

"She did investigative stuff, too. There was this one case in Toronto, the Kraft-Fergusson Brownfield scandal. She won awards for that exposé."

Levon sighed. "Just tell her to be careful, okay? And be sure to tell Merryfield about the houseboat rental."

"Of course she'll be careful. And Luke went to the police right after he told us."

Levon frowned. "Why didn't Luke say something as soon as I'd identified the body as Marc Larroquette? Even if he didn't recognize him, he should have recognized the name."

"That's the thing. He didn't rent the houseboat under that name. He rented it under the name of Kevin Hollister Cartwright."

"Kevin Cartwright. Why does that name sound familiar?"

"He's Emily's ex."

"Right. But why would he use that name? And how did he get Kevin's ID?"

Arabella explained how easy it was to get a Pleasure Craft Operator's Card. "There's no photo on it, and basically you can take the test under any name, once you're online. As for why Kevin, I convinced Emily to meet with him."

Levon chuckled. "So Emily is more than just a little bit involved. You must've twisted her arm."

"A little, but she really wants to help, and to be honest, I think she misses the investigative side of her old job. Anyway, she did meet him in Toronto. Chloe—that's the woman Kevin dumped Emily for

—and Marc Larroquette have a connection. He was her stepfather. Except Kevin knew him as Marc Laurentian."

"Like the mountains in Quebec?"

"The same. He's been living in a place called Goulais River for at least the past ten years and maybe longer. It's about forty-five minutes northwest of Sault St. Marie, in case you haven't heard of it."

"I haven't. I've never been that far north, and I'm sure my mother hadn't either. She was a city girl, and living in the suburbs of Scarborough was like purgatory to her. But go on. You were saying Marc Larroquette, a.k.a. Laurentian, had been there at least ten years. How did you come up with the timeline?"

"That's when he married Chloe's mother, Alice Brampton." Arabella studied Levon's face for any reaction to the name. There was none.

"I've never heard of her, either. Not that there's any reason I should have. My father left us fourteen years before he remarried. It sounds like Emily made the trek to Toronto for nothing. The fake ID with the houseboat rental only shows that he didn't want to use his own name."

"You're wrong, Levon. Marc came to Toronto to see Chloe for the same reason he came to see you—for Face Yesterday, Save Someone Tomorrow. He told her he was ready to face his past and asked her for forgiveness. Alice Brampton had died four years ago in an automobile accident. He said he wanted to make things right with Chloe. I gather he wasn't the best husband or stepfather."

"Some things never change." Levon leaned over and took Arabella's hand in his. "I appreciate what you and Emily are trying to do, but I don't want either one of you to get hurt. Call Merryfield, or your boyfriend, Beecham, and tell them what you've found out. Allow the police to do their job. Okay?"

"Aaron and I are no longer seeing one another," Arabella said, pleased with the way she'd sidestepped Levon's demand. She had no intention of acquiescing.

She had another plan though: find the local chapter of FYSST and join the movement.

20

ARABELLA WOKE up at three a.m. with a pounding headache and a cotton mouth. She knew from past experience that it would take her forever to get back to sleep. She closed her eyes and went over the evening in her mind.

It had started with Levon cracking open a bottle of cognac—a weakness of hers, as he well knew—after serving her barbecued steak, medium rare, just the way she liked it, along with a baked potato, and tomatoes and green beans picked fresh from his garden. It was comforting to know that not everyone in her circle had converted to vegetarianism, although the fact that Levon had a garden surprised her. In addition to the beans and tomatoes, there were cucumbers, zucchini, carrots, and radishes. "I tried growing my own lettuce," Levon had told her with a smile, "but the rabbits kept eating it."

The dinner had been delicious, and was followed by homemade zucchini bread—another surprise. By some unspoken agreement, there had been no more talk about Marc Larroquette- Laurentian or his murder. Instead, Levon regaled her with stories from the road, painting the picture in vivid detail as only he could.

By far the best story was the estate sale in Peterborough. The shelves were overflowing with books, a sure indication that the late owner had been an avid reader. To Levon's advantage, the man's daughters had neither interest in books, nor appreciation for hardcovers, which they deemed "heavy and so nineteen-eighties." Levon offered to take the entire lot off their hands, bookcases and all, knowing that in amongst the Book of the Month Club Sidney Sheldons and Arthur Haileys, there were bound to be at least a couple books worth a few dollars. There was also a solid collection of early Nancy Drews and Hardy Boys, along with some Doc Savage. He paid a hundred dollars for the lot, packed them in his truck, and was gone before the two women could change their minds.

"Let me guess," Arabella said, sipping cognac as the warmth of the liquid seeped down her throat and into her stomach. "There was one amazing find in amongst the bunch."

"More than one. He actually owned half a dozen first editions, all with dust covers intact. No one especially famous." Levon leaned back and grinned. "Well, except for the Ken Kesey."

"Ken Kesey? As in One Flew Over the Cuckoo's Nest?"

"The one and the same." Levon proceeded to tell her about the true first edition. "As you probably know, the book was inspired by Kesey's time working the night shift at a mental hospital. What you might not know is there was a very small first run of the original Cuckoo's Nest, about a thousand copies if I remember correctly. Then a woman named in the book sued Kesey. His publisher, Viking, made him change the character from a Red Cross worker to a man."

"Quite a find."

Levon nodded. "An inscribed copy by Kesey talking about the woman and getting sued sold for over eight thousand dollars at PBA Galleries in San Francisco. The copy I have isn't autographed, so it won't be worth that much, but it should still fetch a hefty sum at the right auction."

Arabella sipped her cognac. She remembered the times when they'd go out picking together, back when they had been a couple. She realized that she missed it. Missed him. Missed them. She wondered if Levon felt the same way. And then he came right out and said so.

"I want us to try again, Arabella."

She forced herself to put on her suit of armor; she didn't have it in her to get hurt again. "You're only saying that because you're in trouble and Gilly Germaine dumped you, snotty bitch that she is."

Levon laughed. "You see, that's what I love about you. No pretense, no BS. You say it like you see it. But in my defense, I was going to ask you last year, around the time when you and Emily were forming a partnership. The timing didn't seem right. The next thing I knew, you were involved with Aaron Beecham. You seemed happy with him. Were you?"

"I was. We were—for a while. He's a good man, kind, honest, hard-working, and obviously law- abiding. But we couldn't get our schedules to mesh, what with his work shifts and me trying to run a retail operation. Emily's great, but like Shuggie, she still has a lot to learn. After a while, Aaron and I just stopped trying. We didn't break up, our relationship just petered out."

Ironically, Arabella and Aaron's biggest argument had been over Levon and Gilly. That was one tidbit she wasn't about to tell Levon. "If you're so over him like you say you are," Aaron had said, "then why do you care about his relationship with Gilly?" Arabella didn't have an answer for that and so Aaron had supplied one. "I'll tell you why. Because, admit it or not, you're still in love with the man, and something tells me that's never going to change."

Arabella and Aaron hadn't broken up that night, but things weren't the same after that. It took longer to respond to each other's voice mail messages and their texts all but stopped. Then one day it just happened—they'd drifted so far apart that it was hard to imagine why they were together in the first place. Nonetheless, Arabella felt a mixture of disappointment and relief, even though she couldn't pinpoint why she felt either emotion, or which one was stronger.

"What about you and Gilly? You certainly seemed hot and heavy before the murder on the golf course."

Levon shrugged. "It was fun, but it was never going to be

serious. Not like it was with you and me. I'm too blue collar for the Gilly Germaines of this world. Maybe if I had my own Pickers television show…"

Arabella laughed at the thought of Levon on TV. The next thing she knew, they were kissing and Levon was carrying her off to the bedroom, and not the spare one he'd made up for her either. She opened her eyes and turned to face her ex-husband, snoring ever so softly beside her. At a time when everything needed to stay simple, things had just gotten a whole lot more complicated.

Y

NEITHER ONE SAID MUCH the next morning over breakfast: bacon, eggs, and home fries for Levon— he'd always been a believer that a liberal dose of grease was the best cure for a hangover—and dry toast and strong black coffee for Arabella.

"We should talk about last night," Levon said while they were doing the dishes, her washing and him doing the drying and putting away.

"No," Arabella said. "No, we shouldn't. Last night was a stroll down memory lane. A very nice cognac-fueled stroll, but not one that we should repeat any time soon. There's too much history between us for it to work."

"What if I don't agree?" His indigo blue eyes stared hard into her green ones.

Arabella fought her desire to drag Levon by his shaggy brown hair right back into the bedroom. "Even if I thought our getting back together was a good idea, our priority has to be finding out who the real murderer is and clearing your name. We can't be distracted by…last night."

"I thought you'd promised to stay out of it and let the police do their job."

Annoyance quickly squashed any additional amorous thoughts. "I don't remember promising any such thing. Besides, Emily needs the diversion. I can't have her moving back to Toronto because she misses the thrill of the hunt. Researching antique sewing trinkets doesn't have the same appeal."

"So what you're saying is that you're going ahead with your ill-advised investigation, even if I don't want you to." Levon's eyes suddenly shifted to icy gray, the way they got when he was seriously irritated.

"I just want to help."

"Then promise me you'll stay out of this."

Arabella stood up and gave Levon a quick hug. "Um… I need to leave now. I have a store to open. Just don't worry about me, okay?" She had no intention of promising anything. She had an investigation to get underway, and no matter what Levon said he wanted, he'd thank her in the end. She decided to start with Nigel Watters, the new owner and resident busybody of the Sunrise Café. If there was anything worth knowing, he'd have the latest scoop.

21

LEVON COULDN'T BELIEVE he'd slept with Arabella last night. What had he been thinking? Well, he hadn't been thinking, at least not with his head. It was true that he still loved her, but she didn't love him back. She'd made that perfectly clear. Her fling with Aaron Beecham should have clued him in—just one more reason why they shouldn't have gotten back into bed together, cognac or not.

But damn, it had felt good.

Was he being a hypocrite? He had been with Gilly Germaine for the past few months. No, on further consideration, he wasn't, because he'd only taken up with Gilly after Aaron had stepped into the picture.

Gilly. She'd certainly made herself scarce since the incident at the golf tournament. That's how he preferred to think of it: an incident. It seemed less personal that way.

Except it was personal. He knew it. Gilly knew it. Arabella knew it. Emily knew it. The police knew it: Merryfield, Beecham, Byrne —three very different cops with the same doubts about his innocence.

Levon shivered, feeling empathy for Samuel Lount, the

nineteenth-century traitor Lount's Landing had been named after. He'd gone to his death unapologetic, his name cleared far too late to save him from the hangman.

Levon couldn't let that happen to him, which was why he hadn't told anyone about the gun.

22

ARABELLA WAS RUNNING LATE, and in her mind for a good reason: she was on a mission. Her first stop, which she temporarily tagged as "home," was at an impersonal midtown rental a brisk twenty-minute walk to the Glass Dolphin that would, finances one day permitting, be replaced with a place of her own. She showered and changed before calling the shop. Arabella was pleased to hear that Emily had already opened and, even better, she was doing just fine on her own. She told Emily that she would be another hour, possibly longer.

"Where are you calling from?"

"Home, and since I'm already running late, I was thinking of stopping off at the Sunrise Café to talk to Nigel. You know what an old gossip he is. I figure he might have heard something."

"So the investigation is officially on. I gather Levon approves."

Arabella chuckled. "Not exactly, but I can't just let him sit around and wait for who knows what.

Anyway, I have a couple of ideas. I'll run them by you when I get there."

"It's not like you to be late," Emily said. "Anything you'd like to share?"

"I'll fill you in when I see you." Arabella hung up before Emily went all investigative reporter on her. As for filling her in, the part about sleeping with Levon last night wasn't a topic open for discussion. She knew Levon would feel the same way.

Arabella did her best to tame her auburn curls, then selected a pair of black capris and a silky tee shirt in muted shades of green and blue. She slipped on a pair of sandals and was out the door, feeling oddly energized by her decision to solve the mystery of Marc Larroquette.

The walk to the restaurant took her past the Main Street Elementary School, a vacant building which had been the cause of three murders in the normally sleepy town of Lount's Landing. It was still up for sale after several months on the market with two different, but unsuccessful, realtors. It appeared the original realtor, Poppy Spencer, had been given another try at the listing.

Word on the street said that Poppy had wined and dined—and possibly a bit more than that—the administrative chair at the school board in charge of property sales and acquisitions. Arabella hoped Poppy wasn't planning to float the mega-box store idea again to another buyer.

Arabella arrived at the Sunrise Café five minutes later. The restaurant was charming in a country- cozy way, with colorful prints of roosters and other farm life adorning the walls. Overhead, ceiling fans with alternating blades of bright yellow and orange spun lazily, circulating the smell of coffee, cinnamon, and buttered toast. Nothing much had changed inside since Nigel Watters had taken it over. Arabella wasn't surprised. He hadn't done anything with Frankie's Fish and Chips when he bought it either. He'd kept the old name, and now he'd sold Frankie's to buy the Sunrise Café. It looked like the new owners were going to keep Frankie's name too. Why pay for a new sign and menus if you didn't have to?

Nigel was reading the latest issue of *Inside the Landing*, the one with the sketch of Marc Larroquette. It was ten-thirty, the calm between the breakfast rush and the lunchtime crowd. His only waitress, Fran, a serious looking woman in her mid-forties with frizzy brown hair tied back with a scrunchie, was busy wiping down tables and setting up menus, napkins, and cutlery for the next wave of customers.

"Hey Fran," Arabella said. "Coffee please, black, and the strongest blend you've got back there." The Sunrise Café didn't have lattes or cappuccinos, but Nigel's addition of select teas and flavored coffees had proven to be popular.

"You got it," Fran said. "Want your usual cinnamon raisin bagel with peanut butter to go with it?"

"Not today. I had some dry toast at...I had some dry toast already."

Fran raised her eyebrows but didn't comment.

Arabella slid into a chair at a table for two, directly across from Nigel. Since he was the cook, it looked like her food would be delayed a while, which was probably just as well. As she expected, he was more than ready to talk.

"Hi Arabella, I heard about the golf tournament. You must have been scared witless, finding that dead body." Nigel spoke from experience, having once discovered a dead body.

"You could say that," Arabella said, then proceeded to satisfy Nigel's gossip tooth, starting with the events at the second hole and the eventual discovery of Marc Larroquette's body at the third. Nigel hung onto every word. So did Fran. She'd kept close enough to hear what they were saying after serving Arabella her coffee, and since the restaurant was empty, had finally given up the pretense, pulling up a chair to listen.

"I had no idea who the man was until Levon came by and identified him to the police. I'd never met Levon's father before. As you know, they'd been estranged." Arabella spoke the last words in a quiet whisper. Seriously, she'd missed her calling as an actress.

"I didn't know until Kerri's column," Fran said.

"Speaking of Kerri St. Amour," Nigel added, "she came in here yesterday acting like she was trying to tell me something, when all she really wanted was to see if I knew anything. Even if I knew anything juicy, I was not about to pass any information to her. There's something about that woman I don't trust."

Arabella was a bit embarrassed since she had come to the

restaurant for the same reason as Kerri, albeit for a nobler cause. She was here to help Levon, not to dig up dirt like Kerri.

"Actually, Nigel, I'm probably not much better than Kerri. Everyone seems to suspect Levon, but I know in my heart he didn't kill his father. I was hoping you or Fran might have seen or heard of something that could help me." Fran seemed to preen at the thought of being a source, while Nigel assessed her with his pale blue eyes.

"Emily is going to help as well. You know how good she is at the investigative stuff."

Nigel nodded. "She's one hell of an interviewer, too." Arabella knew that Nigel was quite fond of Emily. He liked to tell folks they had worked a case together before. Although Emily didn't deny it, the truth was that Nigel's story was more than a bit of a stretch.

"I'm afraid I haven't seen anyone suspicious." He chuckled. "Well, beyond the usual suspects. Chantal Van Schyndle, Caitie Meadows, and Poppy Spencer are my most regular regulars, and all three were at the tournament. From what they told me, the police asked them a few questions, took down their contact information, and then they were free to go. None of them admitted to knowing anything more than what was in the paper or that blog. I believe them."

Arabella had to agree. The most Chantal would be guilty of was overcharging her clientele.

Caitlyn "Caitie" Meadows had been supplying the Glass Dolphin for the past few months with vintage costume jewelry on consignment. Caitie was eternally happy, scrupulously honest, and what she didn't know about costume jewelry made before 1980 wasn't worth knowing. Arabella couldn't imagine Caitie with a gun —unless it was a glue gun—let alone firing it into a man at the golf course. As for Poppy, she would have seen Marc as a possible client and dead men don't buy property. Arabella could understand why the police had lost interest in all three, though it was disappointing that they didn't have anything to add. Then again...

"Chantal and Poppy were in the group ahead of us, which meant they were the first ones at the third hole. Ned was with them, but there was also a guy I didn't know. Miles Pemberton. Do you know him?"

Nigel nodded. "He's from Toronto. Poppy's been seeing him for about a month now. Whether she sees him as a boyfriend or as a potential investor is hard to say. I'm surprised you didn't recognize him though. He's got one of those house flipper shows on TV. Pemberton on Property. He buys fixer-uppers, renovates them, and then sells them for a profit. He's been in here a couple of times. Seems like a nice enough guy."

"Sometimes he renovates with the idea of renting," Fran added. "It's entertaining, though I'll admit I'm addicted to those home shows. From what I can gather, he's been looking at houses with Poppy with the idea of filming one. So far, he hasn't seen anything he likes."

"I'm not much of a TV watcher, so that would explain why I didn't recognize him," Arabella said, "but my guess is that Poppy's interest in him isn't entirely romantic, not that it matters. I don't see him coming up here and shooting Marc Larroquette. And speaking of Marc, did he ever come in here? You saw the sketch of him in *Inside the Landing.*"

"Detective Merryfield asked me the same question yesterday afternoon," Nigel said. "Neither Fran or I remember seeing him, and a stranger would have stuck out."

That was another dead end, though not unexpected. Arabella figured Marc would have stayed close to Lakeside where he'd been renting the houseboat. Primarily a tourist area in the summer, one more middle-aged guy wearing a baseball cap and sunglasses would blend into the background, nameless, faceless.

"There was this man last week," Fran said. "I'm not saying he was a stranger, but he's never been in here before or since. He didn't look like the man in the sketch, though. This guy was your average run-of-the-mill sort, might have been anywhere from thirty-five to forty. Brown hair, brown eyes, medium build."

"Why do you remember him if he was so ordinary?" Arabella asked.

"It was what he ordered. A BLT with double bacon and mustard instead of mayonnaise."

"I remember that order," Nigel said. "Who puts mustard on a BLT?"

"Do you remember anything else about him, Fran?" Arabella asked before Nigel could get into an elaborate story.

"He was on his phone part of the time. He spoke quietly, almost a mumble. I guess he didn't want to disturb the other customers."

Or he didn't want anyone to hear what he was saying.

"I did overhear him saying something about a fist though," Fran said, her face coloring.

Arabella perked up. "A fist. Are you sure?"

Fran nodded. "I remember thinking, that's all we need, a guy with a temper coming in here threatening someone with his fists. But he hung up and ate his BLT without incident. Left me a decent tip, too."

"Would you recognize him if you saw him again?"

"Probably. For sure if he wore the same sleeveless Canada tee shirt. He had a tattoo of a wagon wheel on his upper right arm." Fran stopped. "Now why didn't I make the connection before?"

"What connection?" Arabella and Nigel asked at the same time.

"The tattoo. It was a wagon wheel with five spokes, and there was a letter inside every spoke. F- Y-S-S-T. Fist."

23

Arabella popped into the Glass Dolphin first, just to make sure Emily was doing okay on her own. The store had been quiet, Emily assured her, with just Etta Mills coming by to take still another look at the mission oak sideboard. It was the fifth time Etta had been in to look at it.

The sideboard wasn't Stickley, but it was a fine example of American Arts & Crafts, with original finish and hardware, and it wasn't oversized. It would fit nicely in a small home or condo.

"I think we're getting one step closer to her buying it," Emily said. "Today she asked me if there was any flexibility in the price. Up until now, she's only opened and closed the doors and drawers."

Arabella knew they needed to sell it. Although the sideboard was a beautiful piece of furniture, it had been on the shop floor since she'd opened. On top of that, she'd already discounted all her "brown furniture" by twenty percent—brown furniture being currently out of favor in the market. That said, there wasn't a lot of wiggle room in the price, and she wasn't willing to sell it at a loss. Besides, weren't antiques the original recyclable? Surely she could sell the whole "antiques are green" philosophy the industry had been trying to promote for years.

"What did you tell her?"

"I told her you'd give it some thought and call her later in the week. I don't want her to think we're desperate or anything."

"What did she say to that?"

"She made a comment that it had been here a while. I told her that might be so, but it didn't eat any bread."

Arabella laughed. Emily did have a way of explaining things. "Anything else?"

"I updated the website with a few new photos, including the sideboard—which should get Etta nervous, added a couple more items on eBay, and listed two of the Cunard ocean liner posters on Craigslist." Emily tapped on her keyboard. "Here's the listing: 'Fabulous pair of nineteen-fifties Cunard White Star ocean liner posters depicting the Queen Elizabeth and Queen Mary. Did someone in your family immigrate on one of these ships? Find these and more nostalgia at the Glass Dolphin antiques shop on Lount's Landing's historic Main Street. More photos available. Price on request.'" Emily looked up. "What do you think?"

"We haven't done Craigslist before, but I think it might work. The family tie connection is clever."

"Thanks. I'm going to try and do some more of that sort of thing, especially if this works out. There's a woman who specializes in genealogy that I met at the Women in Business Networking Association in Marketville a couple of weeks ago. She may have other ideas."

Arabella had to applaud Emily's initiative. She would never have thought of the immigration angle, and she wasn't much on networking groups. For the umpteenth time since they'd become partners Arabella thanked her lucky stars for Emily. But right about now, she needed her to do some sleuthing to help Levon.

"It all sounds fantastic. Since you're doing okay, I'm going to head over to Birdsong and pay Ned Turcotte a visit."

"Why Ned?"

"I'll fill you in on everything when I get back."

Emily grinned. "Including why you still have that look of 'I just had great sex last night' on your face?"

"Don't be ridiculous," Arabella said, but she knew her face was as red as her hair. She stomped toward the door and called out before she left, "See what you can find out about FYSST. Maybe there's a local chapter we can join."

Y

BIRDSONG WAS a dozen doors up Main Street from the Glass Dolphin, a narrow store that had the singular advantage of being on the corner of Main and Prince, allowing for windows on both streets. Ned had filled them with an assortment of bird feeders in a variety of shapes and sizes. It was a bit cluttered, but the overall effect was pleasant—a look that carried throughout the small retail space.

Ned had the ruddy-faced complexion of someone who'd spent much of his life outdoors. He was busy rearranging a display of oriole feeders. A sign announced twenty-five percent off. Arabella knew from her days with Levon that oriole season would soon be behind them, the birds starting their migration in August.

Ned looked up, a pleased but surprised expression on his rugged face. "Hey Arabella, what brings you here?"

His curiosity was well deserved since her only visit, aside from today, was in early May to purchase a hummingbird feeder and a jug of nectar. Unfortunately, she was never home long enough to see any hummingbirds. It also didn't help that something—most likely a raccoon—seemed to consume the nectar every night, so there was nothing for the hummingbirds to drink during the day. Arabella had given up after the jug was empty and put the feeder away.

"It's about Levon's father."

Ned nodded. "I suspected as much. I feel bad for Levon. He's a decent man, and he's been a good advocate for the store. I was also upset to read that Kerri St. Amour was trying to pin something on you and Emily. That woman is nothing but a muckraking bitch. Chantal feels the same way."

Arabella knew that Chantal and Ned had been an item for the past few months, an unlikely duo, though whatever they had going on seemed to work for them. Arabella didn't know what Kerri had done to set them off, but it certainly seemed as if the reporter had few friends in the Landing.

"Thanks for your concern. It means a lot."

"What can I do for you?"

"Emily and I are following some leads. We want to clear Levon's name, and our own, of course.

It goes without saying that I want to keep Kerri out of this, as much as possible."

"You two didn't learn from last year's experience?" Ned shook his head. "Merryfield will be none too pleased. Beecham either, for more reasons than one."

Arabella shrugged. "Aaron and I split up a while back. As for Merryfield, I need you to keep this on the down-low. I'll be sure to fill him in on anything he needs to know."

"Why do I think his idea of 'need to know' and yours are completely different? But okay, you've got a deal. I don't owe the police anything. The way he treated me last year—"

Arabella interrupted before Ned could go off on a tangent and filled him in on her visit with Nigel and Fran at the Sunrise Café.

Ned frowned. "I don't remember a guy with a muscle shirt, but there was this Elvis wannabe who came into the shop. He told me he wanted to do some serious bird watching. I sold him a pair of my best binoculars, and he didn't squabble at the price."

"Did he say where he was going to use them?"

"Sorry, no. He didn't talk much at all, beyond asking about the technical aspects of the binoculars. At the time, I thought it was strange. He didn't ask about the birds in the area or the best spots to watch them, but I was happy to make the sale."

"How did he pay?"

"Cash. No paper trail there. He didn't even want a receipt."

Arabella felt a wave of disappointment flood over her. Another lead gone with nothing much to show for it. "Okay, thanks. I suppose I should get back to the shop. I've left Emily alone long enough."

She was almost out the door when Ned called out after her,

"You might check with Betsy Ehrlich over at the Noose. I saw Elvis go in there right after he left the building." He chuckled at his joke. "Get it? Elvis has left the building?"

Arabella laughed—it was kind of funny. Then she headed over to pay Betsy a visit. It was twelve fifteen. She was finally getting hungry, and it was perfect timing to stop in for lunch.

24

THE HANGED MAN'S NOOSE was across the street and two shops up from Birdsong. The pub was nearly deserted, save for three men in suits poring over paperwork while sharing a jug of beer.

The quiet was typical for an early Monday afternoon. Arabella knew she'd have time to chat with Betsy since she did the bulk of her business for the dinner-and-drinks crowd.

Betsy looked up from the bar and a smile lit up her gamine-like face.

"What's the lunch special today?" Arabella asked, swinging herself onto a bar stool.

"Corned beef or shaved deli turkey on rye with a full sour pickle and hot mustard. French fries if you want them."

"I'll have a club soda with lime and the turkey with fries. Do you have any gravy for the fries?"

"I can get Nina to make some." Nina was Betsy's latest short order cook, a tiny woman with shoulder-length gray hair and well-defined biceps; the latter apparently came from her former career of hair stylist.

"Then gravy it is. I need comfort food." And maybe a touch of grease.

"Let me see if the three men over there want to order lunch, so I can get Nina working on everything. After that, I should be able to join you, provided we don't get an unexpected rush. Something tells me you're not just here for lunch."

Arabella wandered about the pub. A passionate local history buff, Betsy had named the pub for the town's namesake, the infamous hanged man, Samuel Lount. Arabella loved the vintage decor, especially the artifacts Betsy had acquired to add ambience and authenticity. She particularly loved the assorted antique clock shelves that lined the walls. Betsy had purchased most of the shelves from Arabella before she'd even opened the Glass Dolphin, and Betsy used them to display all manner of items.

Arabella picked up a rebellion box and admired it. She had looked long and hard for it, and had given it to Betsy as a bar opening gift. Like the other boxes made by prison inmates in 1837 and 1838, it had been carved with a political message about fighting colonial rule and defending Lount: "MAY VENGEANCE DRAW HIS SWORD IN WRATH AND SMITE THE TRAITORS FOR THE DEATH OF MATTHEWS AND LOUNT. TORONTO, AUG. 1838."

Betsy slipped behind Arabella as silent as a cat, startling her. "A guy was in here a couple weeks back. It would have been the Canada Day weekend. I remember the day because he wore a Canada tank top."

If Betsy noticed Arabella's reaction to her mention of the Canada tank top, she didn't show it. "It turns out the guy knew a lot about local history. He came in here because the name of the bar caught his attention. He was fascinated with that rebellion box and offered to buy it. I told him it had been a gift and wasn't for sale, but that he might want to check with you at the Glass Dolphin. He said he was already running late for a meeting in Lakeside, but that he'd pay you a visit another time."

"Thanks for the referral." Arabella knew what Betsy was going to say, but she asked anyway. "Can you describe him? In case he does come in."

"You'd be able to spot him right off. He had this whole Elvis thing going on. Black hair slicked back, big sideburns, a bit of a belly. Not quite Elvis in Hawaii, but close. He had a wagon wheel tattoo on his arm, too, with lettering on it, but it's dark in here and without my reading glasses… anyway, I couldn't make out what it said."

"It spelled F-Y-S-S-T," Arabella said. "It stands for Face Yesterday, Save Someone Tomorrow. It's some sort of organization, group, or cult—I'm not sure which. Regardless, I'm looking for that guy."

Betsy sighed. "I should have known you weren't just here for lunch. This is about Levon's father, isn't it? You'd think last year's experience would have made you a bit more cautious."

Arabella was getting tired of being reminded about last year. It had turned out okay in the end, hadn't it? "I'm being careful."

"If you say so. But what does Rebellion Box Elvis have to do with anything?" A bell rang in the kitchen. "Lunch is ready. Hold that thought."

Y

IN BETWEEN BITES of her turkey sandwich and fries topped with a generous portion of gravy, and the periods when Betsy left to take care of the other customers that walked into the bar to eat and drink, Arabella filled Betsy in on what she'd learned so far: the houseboat rental; Emily's meeting with Kevin; Levon's account about meeting with his father; how Elvis bought expensive binoculars from Ned; and the other guy with the FYSST tattoo, who went to the Sunrise Cafe for lunch.

"Let me get this straight," Betsy said. "Marc Larroquette, aka Laurentian, belonged to an organization called FYSST. He went to Toronto to make amends with Chloe—that's a bit of a mind blower, her connection to Levon—and then to Lount's Landing to do the same with Levon. Next thing you know, Marc turns up dead at the golf tournament. Is that about the gist of it?"

"An admirable summary."

"Do you think Elvis might be the murderer?"

Arabella shook her head. "I don't think so. People will

remember a guy that looks like him. A murderer would want to keep a low profile. My guess is that Elvis was going to Lakeside to meet Marc. I'm not sure how the binoculars fit in. Maybe they don't. Maybe he just wanted a pair and I'm reading too much into it."

"What about the other guy with the same tattoo?"

"I wish I knew, though the reality is he'll be more difficult to find. Fran called him nondescript." Arabella brightened. "She did say that the guy ordered a BLT with double bacon and mustard instead of mayonnaise. Maybe he came in here another time."

"I do remember a guy like that. Who puts mustard on a BLT? But I didn't get his name, and he only came in once."

"Did he have a tattoo?"

"It was earlier in the year. Springtime, I think. He was probably wearing a jacket or a long- sleeved shirt." Betsy sighed. "I'm sorry. I'm not being much help. I can't even remember what he was wearing."

"Do you think you would recognize him if you saw him again?"

"Probably. I'm good at matching faces with orders. You have to be, in this business. Why?"

"Because I have to find one or both of those men. I just don't know where to look."

"I don't know about your guy with the BLT and mustard, but as for Elvis, you might try the Elvis Festival in Collingwood. It's on later this week. A guy like that, he'd probably want to go to the Elvis Festival."

"What Elvis Festival?"

"You've never heard of it? It's in July, been going on for quite a few years. I used to date a guy who was really into Elvis, and he took me there. It was a lot of fun, actually." Betsy sighed. "He was going to take me to Graceland, but I found out he was married."

"How'd you find out?"

"His wife called to tell me. I gather I wasn't his first transgression."

Arabella couldn't help but grin. When it came to men, Betsy's loser radar was legendary. But the Elvis Festival sounded promising.

She put a twenty on the counter—she had to get back to the shop and Google it—then leaned over and gave her friend a hug. "The festival is a great lead. Thank you."

"Just bring me back a souvenir. Something tacky. And stay away from the fried peanut butter and banana sandwiches. Those things will kill you."

25

ARABELLA HURRIED BACK to the Glass Dolphin, anxious to tell Emily everything she'd learned. But first, she wanted to know what Emily had found out about FYSST.

"Not much," Emily admitted. "They do have a website, but it's more of a placeholder, with a password-protected members only section."

"How do you become a member?" Arabella asked.

"There's a contact form to fill out with the usual questions: name, address, how you heard about FYSST, why you want to join. There's no 'About Us' section and no physical address. The Wikipedia entry was just a rehash of the information on the home page, not that I expected Wiki to be a source of information. What did surprise me was today's blog in *Outside the Landing*."

"I haven't seen it yet. What's it say?"

Emily opened the page on her tablet and read. "Chirp, chirp. Why does an antiques shop owner care whether an Elvis look-alike purchased a pair of field binoculars? Could there be more to her inquiries than mere curiosity? And, hey, Elvis, what's with the wagon wheel tattoo?"

An earlier blog had referenced "a little bird." Now "Chirp, chirp." Could it be… "When did the post go up?" Arabella asked.

"About thirty minutes ago. Why?"

"Ned Turcotte was in the foursome ahead of us at the golf tournament, and I left his store about an hour ago. Truth Seeker's chirping birdie has to be Ned. And to think I bought it when he told me Kerri was nothing more than a muck-raking bitch. Honestly, I don't know who to trust any more."

Arabella filled Emily in on everything she'd done and learned that morning. Emily listened attentively, and to her credit, she didn't bring up the subject of last night with Levon again. Arabella was grateful. She didn't want to lie, but she also didn't want to play true confessions. After all, it was just one night. It didn't mean anything.

Did it?

Emily was already Googling the Elvis Festival in Collingwood. "Betsy was right. It's later on this week. It starts on Friday. It says they expect thirty thousand visitors. I have no idea how you expect us to find this guy—not to mention that we can't exactly close the store for that long. And if you think you're leaving me out of this, you have another thing coming."

Arabella paced. She was tempted to bring out the shortbread, but she had two things working against her: a nagging hangover and the sandwich and fries with gravy sitting heavy in her stomach. So much for Levon's grease remedy. She vowed to stop drinking cognac.

"I think opening day is our best bet," Emily said, still navigating the website.

Friday was one of their busier days, not that any day was action-packed. Still, closing the store wasn't a viable option. She toyed with the idea of asking Levon, but he'd want to know why they needed to go to an Elvis Festival. She couldn't think of an answer he'd believe.

"Caitie Meadows has offered to mind the store," Emily said, interrupting her thoughts. "I'm sure she'd be happy to help, if we asked her."

Arabella knew that Caitie hoped to own her own boutique one day, specializing in estate and vintage costume jewelry, as well as pieces made by local artisans. "I don't know," Arabella said. "She doesn't really know anything about antiques beyond jewelry. What if someone wants to haggle with her?"

"We can give her specific instructions. Like she can accept five percent off the sticker price. Or she can phone you and ask if the customer has another offer in mind. It's not like we'll be out of cell phone range. Besides, Collingwood is only a couple of hours from here. We can leave at noon. Caitie would only have to watch the shop from noon until six. Of course, if you don't want to help Levon—"

It was a low blow, but it was effective. "I'll give Caitie a call," Arabella said.

Y

CAITIE WAS HAPPY TO HELP. They negotiated an hourly rate, along with a ten percent commission for anything sold. She arrived at the Glass Dolphin on Friday morning at eleven for a quick run through, eager to prove herself. Arabella remained nervous, but she knew Emily was right. It was only for a few hours, and it would be nice to have another person to trust with the shop.

The trip to Collingwood was uneventful, the worst part of it, as usual, the trek up Highway 400 through Barrie. It always seemed to be busy, regardless of the day of the week or the time of day. Once they turned off and wound their way by Angus and through Stayner, the traffic thinned considerably. They made good time, arriving at the designated parking area by one thirty, and walked up Hurontario Street. They were a little overwhelmed by the throng of people and Elvis impersonators. There were kids as young as five, men as old as ninety-five, and every age in between, donning Elvis's signature outfits: the white sequined bellbottom pants and embroidered jackets. Others wore red, blue, and black versions of the ensemble, equally embellished.

"How are we ever going to find Rebellion Box Elvis here?" Emily asked. "They all sort of look the same, and if he's wearing a jacket, we won't be able to spot the tattoo."

Arabella had to admit it was a problem, and one they should have had the foresight to consider. She was, however, intrigued by the intricacy of the costumes, which featured everything from starbursts to eagles. No doubt, there was some serious money invested. She had an idea.

"There has to be at least one antiques shop in the area. This is a four seasons resort area, after all. Maybe our guy went into it. He wanted to buy Betsy's rebellion box, and he admitted an interest in Canadiana."

Emily checked her phone for antiques shops in Collingwood. "There are a couple of décor-type shops. I doubt those will have the sort of thing we're looking for. It looks like Stayner has a couple of shops, and there's an antiques mall in Thornbury."

They could check Stayner on the way home. Thornbury was the next town west on Highway 26, a twenty-minute drive from Collingwood.

"I think the antiques mall in Thornbury is our destination," Arabella said. "Let's go. We're never going to find Elvis here."

A couple next to her snickered and made their way into the crowd.

Emily was not to be outdone. "It was a bit of a hair-brained scheme," she said to Arabella, and the two of them laughed at that until they were almost in Thornbury.

Y

THE THORNBURY ANTIQUES mall had a decent selection of vendors. "If nothing else, we might find a bargain or two to take back to the Glass Dolphin," Arabella said, wandering the aisles with a purposeful stride. The first step was to find someone who specialized in Canadiana, but in the meantime, she might as well seize the moment.

They ended up buying five boxes of Depression glass and a dozen pieces of blue willow china from a woman holding a going-out-of-business sale in her stall. Judging by the prices, which were already well below retail and still heavily negotiable after that, it wasn't a marketing ploy—she really was going out of business.

"Why are you getting out?" Arabella asked, genuinely curious. She guessed the woman to be in her early sixties. Her braided salt-and-pepper hair, multi-layered prairie skirt, peasant blouse, along with the Birkenstocks she wore lent her the look of an aging hippie.

The woman gave them a sad smile. "I've been in the business most of my adult life. I still remember when antiques were red hot. You could sell anything if it had a bit of age on it. Nowadays, that's not the case. I guess I'm just too old to keep playing the 'one day things will turn around' game. Besides, I've made my money over the years, and I live a simple life. It's time to make it simpler."

Arabella nodded. It made sense. She'd almost forgotten why they were here when Emily piped up.

"We were hoping to find a rebellion box. A friend of ours in Lount's Landing owns a pub, and she has one on display, but she won't sell it."

"Your best bet is to ask Walker Lawrence. He's a Canadian history nut, always going on about early politics." She pointed to a booth that had been curtained off with thick white canvas drapes. "That's his booth over there, but he's closed for the weekend. He's totally into Elvis and what with the Elvis Festival going on in Collingwood…"

The crushed look on Arabella's face must have tugged on the woman's heart, because next thing she was saying, "Tell you what, give me your card. I'll ask Walker to give you a call—no promises."

Arabella fished out a business card out of her wallet and handed it over. "Thanks, I'd appreciate that."

"The Glass Dolphin, 97 Main Street, Lount's Landing. Arabella Carpenter and Emily Garland, proprietors," she said, reading it aloud. "Which one of you is Arabella and which one is Emily?"

They made their introductions, and found out the woman's name was Heidi Jacobs.

Heidi suits her, Arabella thought.

"I might have a few more things to sell you, back at the house, if you're interested," Heidi said. "I promise to leave plenty of meat on the bone for you to make a profit. How long are you ladies planning to stay in the area?"

"We're only here for the day," Arabella said. "We have a friend looking after the shop for a few hours. We're closed Mondays, though. We could come back. It's not a far drive."

"You know, that would work out just fine," Heidi said. "I'll invite Walker over at the same time. He's expressed interest in a couple of my things, and that way you could meet him as well. Why not come around noon, I'll make us lunch. Nothing fancy, though I do make a mean vegetable lasagna, all the veggies fresh from my garden, plus the cheese is from the local dairy."

Arabella couldn't believe their luck. She looked at Emily and could tell she was thinking the same thing.

"We'd love to."

"Good, then it's settled." Heidi wrote down her address on the back of a business card and handed it to Arabella. "Be sure to stop by the local orchard first. Thornbury is apple country, and they make the best apple pie you'll find anywhere. Walker loves apple pie. I'll supply the vanilla ice cream. Homemade, of course."

Homemade vanilla ice cream, market-fresh pie, antiquing, and a chance to meet Elvis. Life didn't get much better than that. Arabella slipped the card in her wallet and shepherded Emily out of there before Heidi had a chance to change her mind.

26

Arabella and Emily stopped in Collingwood on the way home to take in a bit of the Elvis Festival. "These would be perfect for Betsy," Arabella said, holding up a pair of olive green potholders. The potholders had an image of a young Elvis doing the twist in black pants and a tight tee shirt, along with an "authentic" recipe for fried peanut butter and banana sandwiches. Emily laughed. "Just as long as she doesn't add fried PB and banana to the Noose's menu."

Arabella laughed, even though a part of her really wanted to try the recipe. She loved peanut butter and had been known to eat it by the tablespoon right out of the jar. She justified her mini-addiction by only eating all natural, no sugar added peanut butter. Surely Elvis used the kind with added sugar, which made her version healthier. Didn't it?

The drive back was uneventful, although traffic heading in the other direction to cottage country was slow and solid. It was typical for a summer Friday night with folks trying to escape the city for the Muskokas and beyond.

They arrived at the Glass Dolphin shortly after seven to find

Caitie waiting inside for them. She set aside a book on antique clocks and pointed to an empty wooden shelf.

"I sold the black marble clock," she said, a big grin on her face. "The one made in France."

Arabella had to admit she was surprised. It wasn't like clocks were flying off the shelves these days, and the marble clock had gilt pillars, which made it more ornate than was currently in fashion. It was also something you'd never sell online. It weighed a ton.

"That's fantastic," Emily said. "Who was the customer?"

"His name was Windsor Scott," Caitie said. "He told me that he'd been in here before and had bought a couple of things, and that's when he noticed the clock."

"I remember him," Arabella said. "He bought some end tables and a kid's rocking chair, a lot different than a marble shelf clock." She wondered what Windsor Scott's home looked like and what he did for a living. Caitie interrupted her thoughts.

"He said he'd been thinking about it ever since he saw it. I found your book on French marble clocks and we read about it together, and then I searched the Internet and we did some price comparisons. We found a clock that was almost identical—at least from the pictures, but that was in the UK. Mr. Scott felt that your sticker price of five hundred and fifty dollars was fair, but asked if there was any flexibility. I told him I could knock off twenty-five dollars without calling you. Next thing you know, he was pulling out his wallet. He even paid cash."

It was a good sale, Arabella thought, and much needed.

Caitie might dye her hair odd colors—today she had it streaked with neon pink—and her wardrobe was an eclectic mix of cowboy boots, black jeans, rock band tee shirts, and a flurry of colorful scarves. But the fact that she'd taken the time out to fully explore Windsor Scott's interest and was able to get him involved in researching said something about her business potential. She'd do well in a shop of her own.

"That's incredible," Emily was saying. "I've got to try that approach."

Arabella knew that Caitie worked at the local gym weekdays

until eleven, and that she taught Pilates at Chantal's studio three nights a week. The rest of the time, she was working on building up her jewelry business. Given her performance here today, she deserved that shot, and someone had to give it to her. She looked at Emily and the two of them had an unspoken conversation. Emily nodded, smiling.

"Maybe you'd like to work here one afternoon a week, just until you get your own shop," Arabella said. "It would help us out, and you could learn more about running a retail operation. Trust me, there are a lot of quiet days where the only person walking in is looking to use the restroom."

"Seriously? I'd love to." Caitie looked as if she was about to jump up and down. "I know you're closed on Mondays now. Why don't I try opening from noon to six to start with? That way we can gauge if there's any interest, and I can learn gradually."

"It's a deal," Arabella and Emily said at the same time.

"We'll have to get you your own key," Arabella added. "I'll have one made for you tomorrow. That way you can open and close without worrying about us. Emily and I are heading to Thornbury on Monday. We met a woman who's getting out of the antiques business and she's invited us to her house. We bought a few boxes of stuff from her booth today. Sorry to say that I didn't notice any jewelry, but you might try the Thornbury Market sometime. It's not that far to go."

"Thornbury," Caitie said. "I almost forgot to tell you. A man came in just after you two left. He said that Betsy Ehrlich told him about the Glass Dolphin. He wanted to talk to you, Arabella, something about a box. He has a booth in Thornbury, specializing in Canadiana." Caitie pulled a card out of the pocket of her jeans. "He told me he'd been in Toronto for a meeting, and that he was on his way to the Collingwood Elvis Festival. I guess that's why he was dressed like Elvis."

Arabella took the card and laughed when she read the name: WALKER LAWRENCE—CANADIANA ANTIQUES & COLLECTIBLES, THORNBURY, ONTARIO, CANADA.

27

THE GLASS DOLPHIN was unusually slow for a Saturday. The few folks who'd come in were browsers rather than buyers, and Arabella had been antsy all morning. So had Emily. Monday seemed a long way off.

"Stop pacing and have a shortbread cookie," Emily snapped.

"No more cookies. My jeans are starting to get snug."

"If you did a bit more than walk to and from the store every day, you could eat more cookies. Why not go to a yoga class with me? Chantal's classes are quite good."

"I'll consider it." She went back to pacing, then picked up a feather duster and started brushing non-existent dust off the assorted glassware.

"Why don't you give Levon a call? You could go out and keep him company. Tell him what we've learned so far."

"He doesn't need babysitting, he needs to have his name cleared. Besides, we haven't really found out anything yet." Arabella didn't tell Emily that she'd already called Levon. He had been polite, but distant.

She'd put it down to some unease over their evening together when she heard Gilly Germaine's voice in the background. She'd hung up, embarrassed, before he could make up some sort of story, or worse, apologize. That would be the ultimate humiliation.

"I'm going out for dinner and drinks at the Noose with Luke tonight," Emily said. "Why don't you come along?"

"Because three's a crowd."

Emily gave Arabella an appraising look. "Why don't I ask Luke if Hudson can join us? It will be good for us to get out and have some fun."

Arabella considered the offer. A part of her—a bigger part than she cared to admit—really wanted to see Levon again and not just to chat, Gilly Germaine be damned. But she couldn't go down that road again.

Could she?

No, she couldn't. "I'd love to. See if you can set it up."

Y

UNLIKE THE LAST time Arabella had been in the Noose for lunch, the place was packed, every barstool taken, and only a couple of booths left, both with "Reserved" signs on the table. Betsy was behind the counter, pouring drinks and chatting up the regulars. She saw them come in and waved.

"Relax," Luke said, obviously noticing Arabella's worried expression. "I reserved a booth for us.

I know how busy this place can get on a Saturday."

A female server wearing a short black skirt, black nylons, black stilettos, and a blood red V-neck blouse, her fingernails painted to match, seated them. She introduced herself as Lindsay and ran through the specials.

They ordered burgers with sides of Caesar salad and an order of fries and onion rings to split. Emily got a veggie, while Luke, Arabella, and Hudson went for the beef with Swiss cheese. Draft beer—whatever was on tap—for Luke and Hudson, house white for Emily and Arabella.

The drinks were served promptly. Lindsay told them the food would take thirty to forty minutes, due to the crowd tonight, and only Nina on as chef. She left them a plate of bruschetta with a dish of assorted pickles and olives to share—on the house, she assured them.

Hudson started the conversation by regaling them with a story about his latest bookstore signing. "So here I am in the bookstore, and there's a lull, the sort of lull that makes an author feel alone, exposed, and rather pathetic. You can almost imagine a capital letter L for loser tattooed on your forehead. I'm thinking, 'please, someone, anyone come by the table.' I even found myself hoping for a wannabe author looking for free advice without any intention of buying a book."

"People do that?" Luke asked.

"Oh yeah. Probably the same way people go to the Glass Dolphin looking for advice on their antiques without any intention of buying anything in the store. Am I right, Arabella?"

Arabella nodded. "It happens all the time, although I like to think those people might come back and buy one day. What did you do, Hudson?"

"I tried to hand out bookmarks. It's amazing how many people will avoid eye contact just to avoid taking a free bookmark. Finally, an elderly Asian woman comes in and starts walking over to my table, and there's real purpose in her stride. Not my typical target demographic, I grant you, but who am I to judge?" Hudson grinned. "When she got to my table, she pulled out her smartphone and showed me a picture of a Chinese-English dictionary. 'Where find?' she asked, pointing to it."

They all laughed, and Hudson said, "I did what any self-respecting author would do. I took her over to the reference section and helped her find the dictionary. Then I went back to my table and hoped that karma would kick in."

"Did it?" Arabella asked.

"I did end up selling a few books after that. So yeah, maybe. But here's the kicker. I was just about to start packing up when who walks in but Trent Norland."

Arabella sat up straighter. "The hole in one insurance guy."

"One and the same, although thankfully he was wearing jeans and not those god-awful plaid pants.

He said that he lived in the area and heard I'd be there."

"Nice of him to stop by," Emily said.

Hudson nodded, but a frown furrowed his brow. "Maybe, but I got the distinct impression he wanted to tell me something. He made a stab at small talk, bought the first book in my series, and left. I'm probably reading more into it than there was."

Or maybe it had something to do with Marc Larroquette, Arabella thought. She glanced at Emily, who seemed to be oblivious to everything but Luke. She'd talk to her tomorrow when her head was out of the clouds, and get her to call Trent on some pretext.

"What do you think he wanted?" Arabella asked. "Why wouldn't he come to see Luke, or stop into the Glass Dolphin?"

"I don't know," Hudson said. "I put it down to my writer's instinct, but it's probably my overactive imagination. I shouldn't have said anything."

"Here comes Lindsay with our dinner," Luke said. "Let's forget about that day on the golf course, at least for tonight."

If only I could, Arabella thought, and took a generous sip of her wine.

28

THE EVENING TURNED out to be a lot more fun than Arabella imagined. Hudson was handsome and charming, and it was obvious Luke and Emily were totally into each other. She hoped, for her friend's sake, that Luke was the real deal. She knew Emily was still hurt by the way Kevin had broken up with her. Meeting him in Toronto hadn't helped, and her infatuation with Johnny Porter last year had ended badly.

When it was time to leave, Emily whispered to Arabella that she was going to Luke's for a nightcap. "If all goes well, I'll be late tomorrow," she said with a grin.

Hudson and Arabella decided to stay for another drink, Hudson promising to walk Arabella the few blocks home.

"What about your car? Will you walk back here to get it?"

Hudson shook his head. "It's not worth the risk of driving over the limit. I'll call a cab to pick me up from your place." He caught her panicked look. "Don't worry, I'm planning to call for one before we leave here. Luke can drive me back down tomorrow morning. I figure he'll be driving Emily back anyway."

They both chuckled at that, a bit awkwardly, but the moment

passed soon enough. "What's it like being an antiques shop owner in a modern world?" Hudson asked.

"It can be challenging to earn a living," Arabella admitted, "especially in a small town like Lount's Landing. The historic Main Street angle helps, and Emily is really good with the online stuff. We probably sell half of our smalls through eBay, and we've had a few sales of larger items through Craigslist. She writes up the best descriptions. They're filled with all sorts of facts and trivia. I think, sometimes, she misses working as a journalist."

"What about you? Anything you miss?"

"I've wanted to run my own shop for as long as I can remember. It really is a dream come true for me, corny as it sounds. Of course, it would be nice to be making more money."

"It doesn't sound corny to me at all. I've always believed if you do what you love, the money will follow."

Arabella smiled. That's what she believed, too. The money hadn't quite followed her, not yet, but it would. She just had to stay true to the dream.

"What about you, Hudson? What's it like being an author of medieval mysteries in the twenty-first century?"

"Probably not a lot different than being the owner of an antiques shop. I've been very fortunate with my series, but there are plenty of talented authors with great books who are lucky to earn a thousand dollars on a book."

"How can that be?"

"Let's say a book retails for ten dollars. The distributor takes a commission on every sale—the percentage varies depending on the format, i.e. e-book or paperback, as well as the individual distributor, but let's use forty percent as an average. Now, you're down to six dollars."

"Okay."

"Every publisher is different, but some publishers take as much as ninety percent off net sales. Ninety percent, if you can imagine that. Most fall into the thirty to fifty percent range for digital, and fifty to seventy percent for print. Let's be optimistic and say that the author's publisher splits the net in half. That means on a ten-dollar sale, the author is getting three dollars per book. Sell a thousand books, and you're still only looking at three thousand dollars. If the author has an agent, she or he will have to pay them fifteen percent of that, or four hundred and fifty dollars. And the reality is that very few books sell a thousand copies. Of course, there are exceptions, the Stephen Kings of the world. But for every Stephen King there are a thousand authors trying to keep the lights on so they can keep on writing."

Arabella shook her head. "I had no idea. But if it's so difficult to earn a living, why do it?"

"Most authors have a day job, if they're lucky the job has something to do with writing, like teaching creative writing at a local college. But ask any of them and they'll tell you they can't imagine doing anything else but write—just like you can't imagine doing anything else but running the Glass Dolphin, even though the *Antiques Roadshow* moments are few and far between."

"But you don't have a day job. At least…" Arabella blushed. She was getting way too personal.

Hudson smiled. "People think that my Lakeside house is a result of my book sales, and I let them believe it. Perpetuating the myth promotes the whole successful author persona, which in turn generates book sales. The truth is I won some money playing Lotto Max. Not a million dollars or anything, but enough to buy the house, with a little bit left over. I live a simple life, so it works for me."

Hudson took a sip of his beer. "I'm not sure why I'm telling you this. No one knows, not even Luke, and we've been friends for years. There's just something about you that fills me with the need to tell the truth."

Arabella smiled. "My motto is 'authenticity matters.' Maybe you're picking up the vibe. It gets me in trouble sometimes."

"Is that so?"

Hudson leaned over and kissed her softly, first on the forehead, and then gently on the lips, his hands gently cradling her face. Arabella felt herself respond, then noticed Betsy out of the corner of her eye. She was trying to hide it, but there was a definite smirk on her face. She pulled away only to see Shuggie St. Pierre sitting at the bar, grinning like a fool. Damn it. He was bound to say something to Levon. She didn't need this complication in her life right now.

"We should probably order coffee. Or something."

"I'd like an order of 'or something' to go," Hudson said, a smile playing at the corners of his mouth. "But coffee will be fine until we get to know one another a bit better."

Y

TRUE TO HIS WORD, Hudson walked her home, having first arranged for a taxi to pick him up there in an hour's time. Arabella felt an irrational tug of disappointment. She didn't sleep with guys on the first date, or the second one for that matter, and this hadn't even been a date. Sex with Levon had completely messed with her psyche.

They waited on her front porch, reminding Arabella of her days as a pimply-faced adolescent. She could almost imagine her father lurking behind the curtains to see what the boy was going to do next. After an inner debate, she invited Hudson in, but she knew she'd left it too long to come across as sincere. To her relief, he declined, with the proviso that they have dinner together the following week. She accepted, feeling ridiculously happy at the thought.

"I'll call you tomorrow," Hudson said as the cab pulled up. He kissed her goodnight, a soft brush on the lips that hinted of things to come and made her knees go weak. She went inside, chiding herself for reading too much into the evening. At this rate, she was going to have to give up alcohol.

29

LUKE DROPPED EMILY OFF at one o'clock Sunday afternoon, an hour after the Glass Dolphin opened. It was completely out of character for her to be late for anything, let alone work, but she'd been reluctant to leave what had been the perfect date. Luke, it seemed, had felt the same way, insisting on taking her to breakfast at the Sunrise Café. They'd lingered over tea and French toast sprinkled with cinnamon sugar and made small talk, comfortable in the space they'd created together.

Arabella didn't comment on her tardiness, for which Emily was thankful. It also made her feel bad about teasing her friend about her night with Levon. She wondered if they would ever get back together. The timing always seemed to be off for one of them. Still, if it was meant to be...

"I need you to call Trent Norland," Arabella said, dragging Emily back to the present. "The hole in one insurance guy?"

Arabella forced back a snotty comment. "Why is it everyone always refers to Trent Norland that way? Surely by now everyone knows who he is. He even sat with us at the clubhouse."

"Give me one good reason why I should call him when Luke is

handling the administrative side of things, including letting us know that we haven't been entitled to a refund."

"Because he went to Hudson's book signing, and Hudson thought Trent had come there to tell him something, but for whatever reason, he decided not to and left. Remember? Hudson talked about it last night."

Emily felt herself blush. In truth, she had no recollection of the conversation. "Are you saying Trent might have information about Marc Larroquette?"

"I have no idea, but I think it's a lead worth following up. For one thing, it's possible he saw Marc's murderer without realizing it. After all, he would have been at the third hole setting up before the first team of players came out. Since you're the one who dealt with him on behalf of the Glass Dolphin, it would make sense that you would be the one to give him a call."

Emily nodded. "Okay, I can do that, but not today. The office won't be open on a Sunday." Besides, all she wanted to do was bask in the afterglow of Luke Surmanski. Everything else was just noise.

Y

ONCE THE AFTERGLOW WORE OFF, reality set in for Emily. What if her loser radar was leading her astray? She'd felt the same way about Kevin and Johnny Porter, and look where those relationships had gotten her. The more she replayed last evening in her mind, the more she second-guessed herself. For one, there was the way Luke had seemed almost obsessed with what Emily knew about Levon's father.

"Not much," she'd told him, sipping wine on his dock and admiring the way the stars reflected and glittered on Lake Miakoda.

Luke wouldn't let it go. "But you must know something, right?"

She'd sat up straighter then, a warning bell going off in her wine-fogged head. "Why are you so interested?"

"I rented a houseboat to him. I was there when we found him dead on the golf course. Murdered, no less. Forgive me if I'm naturally curious about who he was and what he was doing here."

Emily had bought his explanation at the time. She'd even apologized—blaming her past life as a journalist and for her suspicious nature—and allowed herself to be scooped up into Luke's arms.

Before she knew it, she was telling Luke everything, right down to how Levon blamed his father for his mother's suicide. He'd listened intently, stroking her hair, but never interrupting. At the time, she'd felt comforted. She was also drunk, and the combination of the two dulled her senses to the point that she divulged information about Levon's past, like it was something she had every right to share.

It wasn't until Emily sobered up that she realized she had no right telling Levon's story. Replaying last night's events also got her thinking about Luke's involvement in the whole sordid mess.

Was it really standard operating procedure to rent a houseboat without photo ID and a credit card imprint? Sure, Marc Larroquette had paid cash but even so…

She rubbed her temples to fight off the headache she knew was coming. Somewhere down the line, she'd have to fess up to Arabella.

She wasn't looking forward to it.

30

MONDAY MORNING'S drive to Heidi's house in Thornbury was uneventful. Arabella and Emily stopped briefly at the local orchard market en route. They were surprised at the size of the market, as well as the delectable selection of locally grown, farmed, and baked goods. Even though they were tempted to buy more, they resisted, keeping their purchases to a traditional apple pie to take to Heidi's, and a Thornbury pie—a blend of mixed berries and apples—to take home.

Heidi's place turned out to be a small log cabin with a wraparound porch. A bed of hostas and colorful perennials lined the driveway and surrounded a large, lush vegetable garden, the tomatoes, beans, and peppers hanging like jewels waiting to be picked. Arabella caught a glimpse of the sparkling blue water of Georgian Bay at the back of the property. Or was that considered the front? She always got confused at what was what when it came to places on the water.

Heidi came out to greet them. She wore a purple tie-dyed shirt, circa 1969, a knee-length denim skirt, and leather flip flops. Arabella handed her the apple pie and waved away Heidi's half-hearted offer of payment.

The cabin door opened and a middle-aged man walked out. He wore jeans, running shoes, and a tee shirt depicting a bear chasing the stick figure of a man on a bicycle, the words "Meals on Wheels" above it. His hair was black and slicked back, his sideburns nineteen-seventies wide. This was Walker Lawrence.

Heidi didn't introduce him, and he didn't bother to introduce himself. Instead he said, "I think we've got some business to discuss, in more ways than one. But first we eat, and then we look at what Heidi has for sale. After that, we'll talk about the man you knew as Marc Larroquette." They went into the cabin. The inside walls had been left natural, the logs chinked with mortar, the perfect complement to the wide-plank hardwood floors.

"Reclaimed logs from the Ottawa River," Heidi said, noticing Arabella's interest. "The reason the wood is perfectly preserved is because there is no oxygen or sunlight at the bottom of the river, the factors that cause wood to break down and rot. Gorgeous, isn't it?"

Arabella had to admit the floor was gorgeous. In fact, she wanted to pack her bags and move in. The cabin was perfectly staged: mission oak chairs with well-worn burgundy leather upholstery, a roll-top desk, and a pine harvest table with bench seating. Tapestries, needlework, and quilts hung on the walls. Wooden shelves held an assortment of carved decoys and Black Forest woodcarvings. Cast iron pots and pans hung from the kitchen ceiling. An old-fashioned black cook stove doubled as oven, range, and heat source. There wasn't a glass dish or vase to be seen.

"I know, it's a lot different than what I sell at the antiques mall," Heidi said. "The Depression glass, the Transferware—those things are just business to me. These are the things I have chosen to live with. Until now, none of it has been for sale."

"Why now? Are you planning to move?" Emily asked, and Arabella wanted to kick her.

Sometimes you had to bide your time, not act like an investigative reporter.

Heidi glanced over at Walker and smiled. "Something like that. There are only a couple of pieces I can't bear to part with." She walked over to one of the shelves and selected a small Black Forest carving of a bear. "My late husband gave me this on our fifth anniversary. That's the wood anniversary, if you're into things like that. He was. The rest of the Black Forest carvings hold no special meaning, those are for sale."

"What about the quilts and tapestries?" Arabella asked.

"All for sale, although I don't expect the quilts will have much value beyond decorative. Most of them were made by a local quilter's group, of which I am a member. Projects to keep us busy in the winter. Most of us gave up skiing a few years ago."

Arabella went over to an alphabet needlepoint sampler. It was what was referred to as a schoolgirl sampler, with the name "ANNA, THORNBURY," and the date "1887" carefully stitched underneath the A to Z block letters.

"I didn't realize Thornbury had been established in 1887."

"Actually, the Township of Thornbury was incorporated in 1833," Walker said, "although the town's first business, a milling operation, wasn't started until 1855. By 1857, a stroll through town would have taken you past a general store, a blacksmith forge, cooper and fanning mill shops, grist mills and sawmills, and a post office. And by 1887, the population would have been over twelve hundred people, with many businesses, churches, manufacturing facilities, and banks."

Heidi said, "What makes this sampler truly special is that in 1887 the businessmen of Thornbury, believing themselves to be unfairly taxed, petitioned for independence from the Town of Collingwood, and the Township of Thornbury became of the Town of Thornbury. When our Anna stitched this sampler, local history was being made."

"I knew it was special," Arabella said, "I just didn't realize how special."

"You have a good eye," Heidi said. "Unfortunately, it's not for sale either." Arabella hazarded a guess. "Another anniversary?"

Heidi nodded. "Our thirteenth, the textile anniversary. We were married on Friday the thirteenth, which made everything about it seem magical. Unfortunately, it was our last anniversary. Danny died in a boating accident shortly after."

"I'm sorry."

"It was a long time ago."

"I've been trying to buy that sampler for years," Walker said in an obvious attempt to steer the conversation back to antiques. "It's a wonderful example of Canadian folk art."

"Maybe I'll leave it to you in my will," Heidi said, "along with the Billy Ellis Canvasback decoy you've been coveting forever. But enough about what's not for sale. It's time you take a look around and see if there's anything you want to buy. Walker will stay with you. He knows as much as I do or more about everything in here. I'll pop the lasagna in the oven on very low—that'll give you ninety minutes—and then go outside to sit on the porch. I never could stand watching people go through my stuff, even after all those years of being a dealer."

Arabella understood. She sometimes felt the same way. She waited until Heidi was back outside before making her rounds. She didn't know much about decoys, except that there continued to be a decent market for them. Walker, however, proved to be extremely knowledgeable. She was just about to ask him a question when Emily spoke up.

"How long has she got?"

"A few months, perhaps," Walker said. "I wondered if you'd figure it out."

"It wasn't just that she's selling everything," Emily said. "She seemed to tire just in the short time we were here. Her clothes are loose, as if she's recently lost weight. Her skin color is grayish. The talk of her will confirmed what I'd already been thinking."

Walker said, "She has no living relatives. Her biggest fear is that her things will be sold at the local auction for a song, with a bunch of city people reaping the rewards. When the two of you came to her booth on Friday, Heidi took it as an omen. She still remembers starting out, and Arabella reminded her of herself, twenty years back. So come on, let's see what you can buy. No reasonable offer refused, and some unreasonable offers might even be considered."

"Why don't we start a pile, and you can discuss the pricing with Heidi?" Arabella said.

That agreed upon, Arabella and Emily selected a half dozen decoys, four needlepoint samplers, two Black Forest carvings—one of a St. Bernard and one of a deer—and several quilts. The quilts would fit in with the Glass Dolphin's new local arts and crafts corner, and pay homage to a wonderful woman. Thornbury wasn't exactly local, but it was local enough.

Once they'd made their final decision, Walker went out to confer with Heidi. Truth be told, Arabella wanted everything in the cabin that was for sale, but as it was, they would almost certainly have to leave some of the things they had chosen behind. She knew Emily was thinking the same thing. Their line of credit was always an option, but they didn't like to use it. That was for emergencies. Like if they couldn't come up with the rent.

Walker was back less than ten minutes later, just as the oven buzzer went off. He pulled on a pair of oven mitts and took the lasagna out to cool before turning to the two women.

"How's three hundred dollars sound?"

"It's not nearly enough," Arabella said. "I know Heidi wants to sell everything, but if we paid three hundred dollars, we'd be no better than the city folks at auction."

"You're right, which is why Heidi said you could have the lot for two hundred dollars if you said as much."

"I don't understand. You're lowering the price by a hundred dollars?"

"Uh-huh. Heidi said if you wanted to negotiate, I had to take a few things out of the pile. If you wanted to pay more, then you were the honest businesswomen she thought you were."

"I don't know what to say," Arabella said. "Neither do I," said Emily.

"Just say thank you and pay it forward one day when you're able to."

"We'll do that," Arabella said, and started to cry. Walker put his arms around her and held her close. When she finally lifted her head off his shoulder, she noticed that Emily had gone outside to sit with Heidi. The two of them were holding hands.

31

THERE WAS no talk of business, death, or dying over lunch. The vegetable lasagna was incredible, filled with zucchini, red and yellow bell peppers, and topped with homemade tomato sauce and cheddar cheese from the local dairy. "Most people use mozzarella," Heidi said, "but I find cheddar so much more flavorful."

They all agreed it was delicious, as were the freshly baked rolls, garden salad with fresh herb vinaigrette, and the apple pie, which lived up to expectations and then some. Despite that, it was clear Heidi had run out of energy. She apologized and said she needed to take a nap. "But don't let me stop you. Go on out to the back porch with Walker. It faces Georgian Bay, and the view is nothing short of spectacular. There's freshly squeezed lemonade in the fridge, as well as beer, water, and soft drinks."

Arabella was surprised that she'd almost forgotten the reason for coming went beyond buying antiques for the shop.

Levon.

She couldn't wait to find out what Walker knew about FYSST. But first, they owed it to their host to put things back in order.

"You nap," Arabella said. "We'll take care of the cleanup. We'll be sure to say goodbye before we leave."

It was a good hour before they finally got around to sitting on the back porch, Walker with a can of ginger ale and Emily and Arabella with tall glasses of lemonade. They had done the dishes, put everything away, and loaded the car with their purchases. When they were finally settled, Walker moving his chair toward them, he rolled up his sleeve, exposing the wagon wheel tattoo.

"I started FYSST—Face Yesterday, Save Someone Tomorrow—two years ago. My first recruit was my best friend, Norrie."

Arabella glanced at Emily, who gave an affirming nod that Norrie could have been the guy who'd ordered the BLT with mustard at the Sunrise Café.

"Does Norrie have a passion for BLTs with double bacon and mustard?" Arabella asked. Walker looked surprised. "Yes, but how did you know that?"

"A guy who ordered a sandwich like that at a couple of spots in Lount's Landing had the same tattoo as you. It seemed like a logical conclusion."

"I'm impressed."

Arabella laughed. "You impress easily. Can you tell us Norrie's last name?"

Walker thought about it for a moment and then shook his head. "I'm sorry, no. Confidentiality of the members in FYSST is paramount. I shouldn't even have shared that much."

Arabella was disappointed, but she wasn't about to risk alienating Walker by pushing it. Besides, knowing who Norrie was probably didn't matter. "Can you tell us why you started FYSST? Why Norrie might have joined?"

"That I can do. I wanted to find a way to go back and make amends with folks I'd hurt along the way. Norrie felt the same way, and not because we'd had a drinking or drug problem. Although we'd certainly done our fair share of both along with some gambling, the bigger issue was that we'd been class-A assholes in the way we treated some people in our past. We were young and entitled—you know the type."

"I've met a few assholes in my time," Arabella said with a smile. "Been one, too, on more than one occasion. But this sounds like

AA's twelve-step program, not that I'm familiar with it from personal experience. Is that what you patterned it after?"

Walker nodded. "I've never been to an Alcoholics Anonymous meeting either—I'm not much of a drinker, beyond the occasional beer now and again. But like you, I know about the twelve steps, and did a bit of online research. Step eight is to make a list of all persons you have harmed. Step nine asks that you make direct amends to such people wherever possible, except when to do so would injure them or others. That was when I thought, 'Why does someone have to have a problem with alcohol to take those steps?' And that was the genesis of FYSST."

Except the part about when to do so would injure them or others, Arabella thought. Obviously, something had gone wrong, at least in the case of Marc Larroquette. But she was jumping ahead.

As for Emily, her inner journalist appeared to have taken over. "So initially it was just you and Norrie?" Emily asked. "Or was the plan to recruit more members?"

"We wanted to recruit members from the beginning, but not as a money maker. We set it up as a nonprofit organization."

"Is that the same as not-for-profit? I can't remember," Emily said, but Arabella wasn't fooled. She knew Emily was remembering their "case" from last year and trying to figure out if FYSST was a scam.

"Non-profits are able to do virtually anything a not-for-profit can or can't do, meaning they can't operate with a profit-making motive," Walker said. "The difference is that they can't issue a charitable receipt and they do not need to be registered with the Canada Customs and Revenue Agency. Non-profits range from very high profile groups, like political parties, to small groups of a few people linked by a common interest or cause, like trade groups, professional groups, social clubs, and sporting organizations."

Emily nodded and leaned back in her chair, apparently satisfied with the answer. Walker grinned, as if understanding he'd passed some sort of test. When he started talking again, however, he was completely serious.

"Norrie set up a members-only website. I designed our logo,

making it simple enough to use as a tattoo. We both made up our lists of the people we wanted to make amends to, and in so doing, we hoped to bring others into the fold. That was the second part of the equation, to save someone tomorrow."

Walker paused to take a sip of his ginger ale. "It was harder than either one of us expected. It was difficult to find some people. Contrary to popular opinion, not everyone has an online presence. Some that we did find weren't overly interested in reconnecting."

Emily leaned forward. "Because they were still angry with you?"

Walker laughed. "If only. There were some folks who didn't even remember us. Let that be your takeaway. The transgressions that haunt us are often unmemorable to others."

Arabella's mind immediately went back a few years to a woman named Annie. Originally from Portugal, she worked in the finance department at McLelland Insurance. Pleasant and hardworking, Annie tended to keep to herself, and though she was well liked in the office, she never socialized with anyone during or after hours. It seemed so completely out of character when Annie made a lemon-glazed rum cake for Arabella's birthday. Arabella had been so surprised that she had taken the cake home to Levon, never thinking to share any with her co-workers. It wasn't until Annie left the brokerage and Lount's Landing, that the penny had dropped. Annie had brought the cake in as a way of getting to know her fellow co-workers, and Arabella had been clueless. As far as wrongdoings went, it was pretty minor, but to this day she wanted to apologize to Annie for being so obtuse. She'd tried to find her on Facebook, LinkedIn, Twitter, and Pinterest without success. Arabella wondered if Annie even remembered her, let alone the cake.

Arabella shook off the memory and forced herself back to Walker and the present. Emily was asking him who he'd made amends to.

"That's confidential, Emily, at least for those still with us," Walker said. "However, since he is no longer among the living, I suppose it's alright to tell you that one of those people was Marc Larroquette. At the time I hurt him, Marc was living in Scarborough with his wife, Rita, and his adolescent son, Levon."

Arabella sat up straighter. Levon had always just called her "his mom," never by her first name.

Rita Larroquette. It made her seem more real, knowing her first name.

Walker was still talking. "The next time I saw Marc, he'd divorced Rita, remarried Alice Brampton, and was living a quiet existence in Goulais River with Alice and her daughter, Chloe."

"If he moved and changed his name, how did you find him?" Emily asked.

Walker smiled. "I'd like to tell you it was my impressive sleuthing skills, but the truth is, it was a coincidence. I had camped at Pancake Bay Provincial Park so I could hike the nature trail up to where the Edmund Fitzgerald sank back in 1975. I've been fascinated by that shipwreck since the first time I heard Gordon Lightfoot's song, The Wreck of the Edmund Fitzgerald. The path leads to a long, winding bunch of stairs to get to a lookout platform."

"Can you see the shipwreck?" Emily asked.

Arabella shot Emily a "what are you doing" look that both Walker and Emily ignored.

"You can't see any evidence of the wreck," Walker said, "but there is a commemorative plaque. You can also see the wide expanse of Whitefish Bay, and it's not hard to imagine what it would have been like that icy day in November out on Lake Superior. Anyhow, there I was at the top of the point when who walks into the lookout but Marc Larroquette with the woman I now know to be Alice. Time had been kind to Marc. He was still lean, and outside of some gray hair, he looked pretty much the same."

Walker chuckled, patted his belly, and ran a hand through his slicked back black hair. "I can't say the same held true for me. I'd always liked Elvis's music well enough, but it wasn't until I joined an Elvis tribute band as a piano player that I started dressing the part. That was about eight years ago. We play the occasional wedding for friends and family, but it's more about having fun than making a living."

Arabella tried not to fidget. Walker would tell his story in his own way, and interrupting him was not going to speed him up.

He finally got back on point. "So, I was thinking, maybe I don't want Marc to be reminded of our history. I tried to leave without drawing attention to myself. I still wanted to make amends, but I wanted it to be in a safer place. One not quite so high up and isolated."

Walker paused and took a sip of his ginger ale, his hand trembling ever so slightly. "You see, it's my fault that Marc Larroquette left Levon and Rita."

32

Emily guessed at the truth. "You had an affair with Rita Larroquette." Her tone was matter-of- fact, but Arabella detected an undercurrent of anger it in. It was understandable, given her history with men who had cheated. Arabella could commiserate.

"If only it were that simple," Walker said. His hand had stopped trembling and he seemed to have regained his composure.

Emily was now every bit an investigative reporter. "What could have been so bad that whatever you did made Marc Larroquette leave his wife and son, change his last name, and move eight hours north to a remote town like Goulais River?"

"I mentioned before that I'd done some gambling. It was actually more than 'some.' There was a time when gambling was how I made my living. Norrie, too, which is how we became best friends in the first place. When the horses were running at Woodbine, Greenwood, Mohawk, or Fort Erie, we'd both be there, program in hand, trying to beat the odds. Did the horse have a history of breaking? If it was raining, was the horse a mudder? If my calculations didn't pan out, I'd start betting on the jockeys, instead of on the horses they were riding. Some nights I made out like a bandit."

"Some nights," Emily said. "I'm guessing that there were a lot more nights that you didn't make out nearly so well."

Walker nodded. "That's the nature of the gambling bug. If you win, you keep on betting like you're never going to lose. And if you're losing, you keep on betting because your luck has to turn around sometime. One of my favorite tracks was the Greenwood Racetrack in Toronto."

Emily frowned. "I grew up in Toronto. I don't recall a Greenwood Racetrack."

"You're probably too young to remember it. It was located on prime land, at the foot of Lake Ontario and Woodbine Ave. The land was sold and the clubhouse was demolished in 1994 to make room for housing and commercial properties. But back in the day, Greenwood was like a second home to me."

Arabella wanted to strangle Emily. They would never get to the story if she kept interrupting with inane questions about racetracks. Then again, Emily was a seasoned journalist. Maybe this was how you got the full story.

Walker continued. "I first met Marc at Greenwood. You got to know the regulars pretty quickly, and Marc was more regular than most. Unlike some guys, who would stand up and shout for their horse, Marc would sit there, composed, program in one hand, ticket in the other. If his horse won, he'd calmly get up and go to collect his winnings. If his horse lost, he'd rip up his ticket in four pieces and toss it on the concrete floor with the rest of the losers. The only sign he'd lost big or small was the color of his face. A big loss and his face would go chalk white."

Walker stopped long enough to take another sip of his drink. "It was a night when he lost every single race. That happens, sometimes, same as the nights you can't seem to do anything wrong. That night, I had the magic touch and could do no wrong, but I could tell by Marc's pallor that he was betting bigger—and losing bigger—with every race. The night wasn't over yet, the final trifecta still had to run."

"What's a trifecta?" Emily asked.

"It's a race where you bet on the horses that will come in first, second, and third in a single race. The idea is to box them, in other words, bet every permutation of that combination, so your three horses can come in first, second, or third in any order and you'll still win."

"Is that expensive?" Emily asked.

Arabella was torn between throttling her and wanting to know the answer herself.

"It's certainly more expensive than placing a single bet," Walker said. "Essentially, you're tripling your wager to cover all the odds. So boxing a two-dollar bet on three horses would run you twelve dollars. But if you can't afford to box a daily double or an exactor, you're better off not to bet the race. Trust me, it hurts like hell when the horse you picked for first comes in second and the horse you picked to come in second comes in first…and you haven't covered that possibility."

Arabella suppressed a grin. Spoken like a true gambler. She'd likely place a two-dollar bet and take her chances.

"Let me guess what happened," Emily said. "Marc hit you up for a loan. You'd gotten to know each other a little bit over the weeks, and he wanted to box that trifecta."

Walker nodded. "He knew I'd been winning and winning big. He, on the other hand, had reached the point of desperation. He asked me for five hundred dollars."

"Five hundred dollars," Arabella said. "That's a lot of money to ask for, especially from a virtual stranger. Did you give it to him?"

"Norrie thought I was crazy, but yes, I did."

"Wow, you're trusting," Emily said.

"I'm a gambler, remember. Besides, Marc considered me a friend."

"Did he win?" Arabella asked.

Walker laughed, but there was no humor in the sound. "Of course not. You don't turn your luck around by throwing good money after bad. A friend would have refused to give him the money. A friend would have told him to cut his losses and go home, to come back another day when the racing gods were on his side.

Then again, I wasn't his friend. Marc Larroquette was about to find that out the hard way."

33

WALKER SIGHED. "To this day, I don't know if Marc put the entire five hundred dollars on that trifecta, but I do know that his horses didn't come in. He'd picked three long shots, and to be fair, the long shots were coming in that day. If he had won, he'd have made a bundle.

Unfortunately, the favorites came in—one-two-three—just the way the odds-makers had predicted. There wasn't even a photo finish, and the long shots were left swallowing their dust."

"Weren't you worried about getting your money back?" Arabella asked.

Walker shook his head. "He offered me his wedding ring as collateral but I turned him down. This was a guy who loved the horses as much, maybe even more, than I did. There was no way Marc would avoid the track in the future, and he knew he'd run into me eventually."

"Let me guess," Emily said. "You weren't being nice. You knew you had him if you didn't take him up on his offer."

Walker flushed but held Emily's gaze. "Yes. I'm not proud of who I was then."

"You said you were the one responsible for Marc leaving Levon and Rita," Arabella said. "What happened next?"

"It was every bit as tawdry as you might imagine. After that day, Marc's luck had run out. He kept coming to the track, and kept losing. I could tell by the sick look on his face that he was betting more and losing bigger, though to his credit, he did pay me back the week after he borrowed the five hundred dollars. I never asked him where he got the money, but I noticed that he stopped wearing a watch and his wedding ring. I suspect he went to a pawnbroker."

Arabella sat back in her chair, thinking. Did Levon know any of this? She didn't think so—in fact, she was pretty sure he didn't. But when it came down to it, was Levon any different than his father? True, he didn't gamble on cards or horses, but being an antiques picker was a bit like being a gambler. You never knew what was going to be a hit and what was going to sit in inventory until you all but gave it away. If that wasn't gambling, what was? And how many times during their marriage had Levon spent money they didn't really have on a perfect "find?" Then again, hadn't she done the same thing with the Pottageville purchases?

"A pawnbroker," Emily was saying. "I can't imagine a family living in a blue collar section of Scarborough would have a lot of pawn-worthy goods to support a gambling habit."

"You'd be right," Walker said. "It wasn't a month later when Marc asked me if I knew of any poker games. The horses were done for the season, and he needed a way to recoup his losses. He'd told Rita that he'd been robbed at the racetrack parking lot and that they'd stolen his ring and watch and wallet. He wanted to buy it back and tell her the police had found it and called him."

"Did you know of a poker game?" Emily asked.

Walker nodded. "I did. I also knew from personal experience that these weren't guys you wanted to owe money to."

"And yet you sent him anyway," Arabella said.

"Yes. It was my way of paying off a sizable debt of my own. I'd gotten in way over my head with a game in Agincourt. If I could send in another rube, they would forgive the exorbitant interest accumulating daily and let me off with paying back the debt plus ten points." Walker shrugged. "I did warn you I wasn't the nicest guy back then."

"You did," Arabella said, "and we aren't judging you." *Well, maybe we are,* Arabella thought, *but he doesn't have to know it.* "So what happened next?"

"Marc went to the game, on my recommendation. He won the first two nights, but that's how these guys hooked you in. Then, when you were sure they were legit and you could trust them, they brought down the hammer. Remember that line in The Sting, where Paul Newman, as Henry Gondorff, is playing poker on the train with Doyle Lonnegan? The audience knows that Lonnegan is cheating, and Gondorff is out of luck. And then he comes up with four jacks and says—"

"You owe me fifteen grand, pal." Arabella said, mimicking Paul Newman's half-smile. "The Sting is one of my all-time favorite old movies."

Walker winced at bit at the "old movie," then grinned. "Remember what Lonnegan says next?"

Arabella didn't miss a beat. "'What was I supposed to do? Accuse him of cheating better than me?'"

Walker's grin faded. "Playing with those guys in Agincourt was a bit like that, except that this was real life. Unfortunately for him, Marc accused them of cheating and made it clear he would spread the word to anyone who would listen. Let's just say the boys didn't take kindly to that. They made sure that Marc made good on his losses—after a little persuasion."

"They beat him up?" Emily and Arabella, together.

"That would have been the easy way out, at least for Marc," Walker said. "No, they threatened to hurt Rita and Levon if Marc didn't leave town. Leave town and never come back."

"And so that's what he did," Emily said.

Arabella's mind drifted to the day she'd caught Levon arguing with his father in the park. He'd admitted later that the argument had been over his mother's suicide, but never once did he speculate on the reason why. Now she realized they had been arguing over his mother.

Damn Levon. How much did he know? And why wasn't he saying anything?

34

ARABELLA WAS STILL PROCESSING everything Walker had told them, and what Levon might possibly know and not be telling her, when Emily went into full reporter mode.

"Great background on Marc Larroquette, Walker, but you didn't tell us when the two of you spoke, and how you ended up recruiting him into FYSST."

Walker grinned. "I wondered if one of you would ask about that. Marc recognized me at the lookout. Instead of being angry with me, he thanked me for saving his life."

"He thanked you? I wasn't expecting that," Arabella said.

"Nor was I. We agreed to meet for lunch at a restaurant in Sault Ste. Marie the following day. I'll admit I was nervous. What if he actually harbored a grudge all these years and had some plan to get even? I needn't have worried. He told me that leaving Levon and Rita had been the hardest thing he'd ever done. Because of that, he swore off gambling and hadn't played so much as a friendly game of euchre since. He'd even stopped watching all sports because he worried he'd give into the urge to bet on the game."

"And he moved to Goulais River," Emily said.

"He figured it was far enough away that no one would find him, and he was right. After a couple of years, he met Alice Brampton, a single mom with a daughter named Chloe. They married, although Chloe never really accepted him in the role of stepfather. Marc admitted he was far from being a perfect husband and father. To say his relationship with Chloe was strained would be an understatement."

That tallies with what Kevin told me, Emily thought.

"Did he know about Rita's suicide? About Levon's time at the young offender boot camp?"

"He did, but according to him, it was several years after the fact. I'm not sure exactly when or how he found out—he was very vague about that—but he told me that it haunted him."

"Not so haunted that he did anything to make it right," Arabella said.

"How do you make someone's suicide right? How do you make walking out on your wife and kid right, even if you had the best of reasons?" Walker asked. "Regardless, I don't think he tried overly hard to reconnect with Levon. In many ways, Marc was a coward. The bravest thing he'd ever done was leaving Rita and Levon. Facing that past terrified him. That's when I told him about FYSST. He listened. By the end of lunch, he asked if he could start a Northern Ontario chapter."

"So you believe his interest in FYSST was sincere?" Emily asked.

"I believe he wanted to make amends with Chloe and Levon, and I suspected there may have been others on his list. Heading a Northern Ontario chapter of FYSST would give him the excuse he needed to approach them. I tried to warn Marc to be careful. My own experience had taught me that not everybody embraces the concept of forgiveness. Some things truly are best left buried in the past."

Y

EMILY AND ARABELLA left a short while later, their good-byes filled with heartfelt thanks to Heidi for her generosity and a promise to visit again soon.

Arabella asked Emily to drive so she could think. She was disappointed that Walker didn't have much to add in the way of current developments. All he knew was what Marc had told him, that he was going to try to make amends with those he'd wronged in the past as his first step in the FYSST program. Chloe and Levon were a given. As to who the "others" might have been, either Walker didn't know or wasn't saying.

Could the others be the poker players that sent Marc packing all those years ago? Walker didn't think so, and Arabella was inclined to agree with him. Marc had repaid the debt and left town. Those had been the terms, and they had been fulfilled. Arabella bit her lip and tried not to cry. No matter which way you looked at it, Levon remained the prime suspect in his father's murder.

Walker had not yet gone to Detective Merryfield with the story, saying he hadn't done so because he still harbored remorse for his role in Marc leaving Rita and Levon. He wouldn't intentionally cause Levon any more difficulty, at least not as long as he believed in his innocence. But if he believed that Levon was guilty, even for a moment, he wouldn't hesitate to come forward. Walker had also made that much very clear.

The more she thought about it, the more she was convinced that Levon knew about Marc's real reason for leaving him and his mom. Maybe he hadn't at the time, though perhaps even that was suspect, but he knew before Marc died.

It would be better for Levon to see Merryfield and tell him the rest of the story before someone else did. Just how she was going to convince her stubborn ex-husband of that was another matter. Maybe if Emily could dig into the past—beat Kerri to the punch to find out the facts—Arabella could confront Levon and show him how it was bound to come out eventually. "Get in front of the story," that's what PR firms always tell people to do, isn't it? Arabella's thoughts raced faster than a thoroughbred at the Kentucky Derby.

"I know what you're thinking," Emily said. "You're worried that

Kerri Say-no-more will get wind of what Walker told us, and if she reports it before Levon tells the police, he's likely to be charged with murder."

"That's the gist of it."

"If it's any consolation, I don't think he will. He's not the type to go running to a reporter. If he talks to anyone, it will be Merryfield."

"I'm not worried about Levon talking to Kerri. Regardless of what you think about her, Kerri is a good investigative reporter. She'll look for the same leads that we have. What if Kerri digs into the past and finds out on her own?"

"If Levon didn't know the real reason his father left, how is Kerri going to find out?"

"I think Levon probably knew."

"You could be right," Emily admitted, "but would she follow that trail? Walker didn't remember the names of the poker players."

"Didn't remember or wasn't telling us?"

Emily shrugged. "It doesn't much matter either way. If he remembered their names and chose not to share them with us, then I don't see him telling Kerri."

"You're probably right."

"There's no probably about it. Now chill out and start acting like someone who just scored a great deal for the Glass Dolphin. The last thing we need is Caitie thinking there was any reason for our trip other than an antiques shopping expedition." Emily tapped her fingers on the car seat. "If Kerri even gets a whiff that you're playing private investigator, she'll be on it. Her newspaper articles might be factual, but that won't stop her from blogging."

"We're playing private investigator," Arabella said, with a smile. "It's not just me, you're in this too."

"Don't remind me. The last time you got me mixed up in a murder, I almost wound up dead."

35

CAITIE'S DISAPPOINTMENT was evident when Arabella and Emily arrived at the Glass Dolphin. "The shop has been dead quiet, not a single customer," she reported.

"No real surprise. We've always been closed on Mondays," Emily said. "I haven't even updated the website yet. I'll do that tomorrow and get the word out on Facebook and Twitter."

"You should set up a Pinterest account, too," Caitie said. "I've sold some jewelry by putting photos on Pinterest with a link to my website."

"Pinterest is a great idea. Why I didn't think of it?"

"You would have. Anyway, there were no customers, but there was one visitor. Constable Beecham came by to see Arabella. I told him you were on a buying trip with Emily."

Why would Aaron want to see me? Arabella suspected it wasn't a social call.

"Maybe he wants to get back together with you," Emily teased, but Arabella knew she was only doing it for Caitie's benefit. They both knew the odds of them dating again were negligible.

"Did he say anything about the reason for stopping by?" Arabella asked.

Caitie shrugged. "No, but it's probably about the guy they found dead by the golf course this morning, the insurance guy?"

"Trent Norland?" Emily and Arabella asked at the same time.

"Yeah, you should read *Outside the Landing*." Caitie looked sheepish. "There weren't any customers and that blog is my guilty pleasure."

"We'll unpack the car first and I'll give him a call."

Arabella needed a few minutes to think. Trent was dead. What would Aaron want to ask her? "I take it the trip was worthwhile?" Caitie asked as they lugged boxes in to the shop.

"It was incredible," Emily said. "The woman who owns the place, Heidi, was more than fair in her pricing, and we ended up with more than we thought we'd be able to afford. You have to see what we bought."

They unpacked the boxes, answering Caitie's questions as they found space for their finds in the already crammed room in the back that they used to store inventory that was not yet priced.

Caitie left to teach her Pilates class and Arabella was dialing Aaron Beecham when the doorbell chimed. Arabella checked her watch and thought, a customer at five o'clock on a Monday?

"Yoo-hoo! Anyone in?" Kerri St. Amour's voice rang out. "Oh, there you are, hiding out back." She strutted toward them in a bubblegum pink sweater that barely skimmed her upper thigh, skintight black jeggings, and five-inch burgundy stilettos. The fact that she rocked that ridiculous look only aggravated Arabella. She could only imagine how Emily felt.

"We weren't hiding," Arabella said, trying not to sound churlish. "We were working. We just came back from an antiques shopping trip and were sorting through our finds."

"Not that it's any of your concern," Emily said.

"What can we do for you?" Arabella asked, hoping to avoid an incident while resisting the urge to drive Kerri right into next week.

"Seriously, do you treat all your customers this way? No wonder business is bad."

Arabella bit back a retort and shot Emily a warning glance.

They could not let Kerri get the better of them. "Where are you getting your information? Business is quite robust."

They all looked at each other for a moment. Finally Kerri said, "I'm here because I wanted to get your reaction for *Inside the Landing*."

"Our reaction to what?" Arabella asked, playing dumb.

"Why, to Trent Norland's death, of course. You know, the hole in one insurance guy, the one who was covering the jet ski promotion for the Glass Dolphin."

"We are aware of who Trent Norland is," Arabella said. "What about him?"

"A dog walker found Trent's body early this morning on the Miakoda Trail, which runs directly behind the golf course. He died of a gunshot wound to the chest, just like Marc Larroquette. Of course it's too early to know if it's the same gun, but the similarities are obvious."

"Where on the trail?" Emily asked. "By the third hole."

The hole where Marc had been shot, Arabella thought. Why had Trent gone back there? What or who was he expecting to find?

"Do the police have any leads?"

Kerri smirked, clearly savoring the moment. "As a matter of fact, they do. They dredged the pond on the third hole of the golf course. Amongst the lost balls was a gun. The police believe it's the murder weapon."

Arabella braced herself for what had to be coming. She knew, of course, that Levon owned a gun. But it wasn't the type of gun you shot someone with. It was an antique gun, an 1883 Enfield revolver. She remembered the way they'd argued about it when he bought it. Arabella hated guns. Levon had told her she was being ridiculous, that it was a collector's item.

"Do they know who the gun belongs to?" Emily asked.

"Those details are being withheld for the moment. However, I know that it's an antique gun. 'An Enfield revolver,' Detective Merryfield said."

"Had the gun been fired?" Emily asked and Kerri hesitated for a split-second.

"I…that information is being withheld, too. But naturally when I heard 'antique' and 'gun,' I thought of Levon, especially since you don't need a license in Ontario to buy, sell, or own antique firearms. It's the sort of thing an antiques picker would know and own, isn't it?"

"Why don't you ask him?" Arabella said.

"I'd love to, but it seems he's up and disappeared. He's not answering his cell, either. You two wouldn't know where he is?"

"We do not." *And we wouldn't tell you if we did*, Arabella thought, but her heart was pounding and there was a knot inside her stomach with an anchor attached to it.

Where the hell had Levon gone? And how did his gun end up in the pond?

36

ARABELLA CALLED Levon's cell phone the minute Kerri left—not a moment too soon. She listened while it went to voice mail, then left a message for him to call her and started pacing. Where could he be? Perhaps Gilly Germaine had heard from him. But what would she say to Gilly?

"Hey there, I'm looking for my ex-husband and wondered if you knew where he was?" Ridiculous.

Arabella also knew she should call Aaron Beecham, but she didn't feel up to a thorough grilling.

She was still mulling over possibilities when Emily spoke up.

"I should have called Trent when you asked, not made up a bunch of excuses. I had my head so wrapped up in Luke Surmanski that I'd all but forgotten about Levon."

"It's not your fault. Like you said, Trent's insurance office wouldn't have been open on the weekend, and today we were off antiquing in Thornbury. The question is, why was he on the trail behind the third hole of the golf course? Blaming ourselves, or each other, there's no percentage in that."

"What about the gun? Do you think it might be Levon's?"

"I wish I didn't, but it sounds exactly like the gun he bought a few years ago when we were still married." She told Emily about their argument, and how he'd told her it was a collector's item, and not a weapon.

Emily was already tapping away at her keyboard. "He was right, not that there was ever any doubt. According to Wikipedia, the Enfield Mark I and II revolvers were used in the British Military from 1880 through 1887, and issued as side arms for the North-West Mounted Police in Canada from 1883 until 1911." She looked up. "Maybe Levon sold it. He is in the business to make money, after all."

Arabella brightened at the thought. It was possible. "Are you going to call Aaron?"

"Not right now. I'll wait until I get home." Whenever that might be. She needed to find Levon first. To find out if he'd sold the gun, and if not, how it had landed in the pond.

Emily walked over to an oak roll-top desk, opened the bottom drawer, and took out a yellow legal pad and a pen. "We could make a list of possibilities. For the murder. Not for the gun."

"I suppose it's worth a shot. Oh god, did I say that out loud?"

"Let's just start."

Continuing to think aloud, Arabella blurted out, "Okay, I'll start. What if Trent was the one who shot Marc and went back to make sure he hadn't left any evidence behind?"

"And in so doing, shot himself? Seems unlikely."

"You're right. Don't write that one down."

"I wasn't planning to," Emily said with a smile. "Any other ideas?"

"What if Trent thought he saw something or someone, and went back to see if he could find anything to support that?"

"You'd have to think the police checked the area pretty thoroughly." Arabella sighed. "What do you think happened?"

"I think Trent Norland must have seen someone or something while he was waiting for the first team of golfers. What if he arranged to meet with the person at the scene of the crime?"

"Why would he do that?"

"Blackmail? There can't be a lot of money in selling hole in one insurance in Ontario. We have a maximum of six months of golf, and you have to figure most tournaments run from May through September. Five months to earn a living."

"Fair enough. Let's surmise that Trent needed money badly enough that he was willing to blackmail someone for it."

"Hudson had the impression that Trent wanted to tell him something, but didn't," Emily said. "True, but I can't see him trying to blackmail Hudson."

"You were the one who thought he might have been Luke's accomplice."

"And you were the one who mocked me for thinking it. Besides, he did donate a signed first edition of his first two books, and a name-a-character in his next book."

"Yes, but that doesn't mean he was in the silent auction room. Your earlier instincts could have been right." Emily tapped the pen against the legal pad. "Are you sure Hudson didn't have any inkling of what Trent wanted to tell him?"

"It was just a feeling Hudson had. He called it his 'writer's instinct.' I'll give Hudson a call tomorrow. We're supposed to have dinner again this week, so it won't come out of the blue."

Emily grinned. "Aren't you becoming the heartthrob?"

Arabella blushed. "It's not like that. Anyway, back to Trent. I think you're right. He went to the golf course to meet someone. Blackmail seems as likely a reason as any."

"Whatever the reason, my guess is that whoever he met there is the killer. All we have to do is find out who he met."

"Is that all?"

"No, that's not all. We also have to hope he wasn't meeting Levon."

"You don't think Levon is guilty, do you?"

"Of course not, but you have to admit it doesn't look good, him doing a vanishing act." Arabella was forced to admit it did not. But she did have an idea of where he might have gone.

37

ARABELLA TOLD EMILY she was going home for the night, knowing full well she had no intention of doing so. It wasn't that she didn't trust Emily; it was more like she was protecting her. At least that's what she told herself.

"Sounds like a plan," Emily said. "I'm exhausted. See you in the morning?"

Arabella nodded. "I might be a bit late. I forgot to tell you that I had a dental appointment. With the dentist."

"A dental appointment with the dentist. That's certainly better than a dental appointment with a veterinarian." Emily eyed Arabella with suspicion. "What are you actually planning?"

"Nothing. And I could have had a dental appointment with the hygienist."

"Whatever you say. I'm tired and my imagination is in overdrive. I'll see you when you get in. Do you want me to sort the quilts and hang them on the quilt racks you have stored in the inventory room? I can get some descriptions written and make sure to promote the local angle. Plus, it will make for some new Facebook and website content. I'm going to try Caitie's Pinterest suggestion, too. The quilts can be my first board."

"What about Etsy? Who was the woman who specialized in lampshades with matching pillows?

She left her card with me, said Etsy was her best resource."

Arabella went over to her desk and opened a drawer filled with business cards. "Here it is. Leah Clark, Leah's Shades and Shams. She uses fabrics designed by Ralph Lauren and Laura Ashley, among others. Really pretty stuff. We weren't sure if her stuff would be a good fit, but now that we carry quilts...not that I know how we're going to price them."

"Etsy is a great idea. Leah might be able to help with pricing, or she might know someone. Don't all those sewing types know each other?"

Arabella grinned. "I'm not sure that they do, but it's a good suggestion. I'll see you in the morning."

"That you will. After your...dentist appointment."

Arabella was almost out the door when Emily called out to her.

"Be careful, Arabella. And say hi to Levon for me when you find him."

Busted. Arabella would have laughed except this was no laughing matter.

$$\Upsilon$$

THE OLD COUNTY ROAD leading to Camp Miakoda twisted and turned at random, as if whoever had designed it had no sense of direction. Arabella was tempted to drive over the speed limit, but she'd gotten a ticket here last year and wasn't in any hurry to repeat the experience.

Arabella checked her watch when she got there. Six-thirty. Still a good two hours before sunset, but she'd have to hurry. It wasn't like there would be any streetlights. At least she'd had the foresight to bring a flashlight, not that she relished the idea of walking the winding, wooded trail in the dark. She shivered despite the heat, thinking of what sort of wildlife might be out there. Coyotes, without question. Foxes, most definitely. Probably moose and deer. Black bears.

Levon's car was nowhere in sight, but that didn't mean he wasn't here. There were plenty of other places to enter the camp, places along the river, or if you were able to navigate the woods like a tracker, a mile or two down the road. She'd meant to check at the old hydro dam and forgot. She parked as far away from the road as she could, hoping her vehicle wouldn't be visible to anyone driving by. It wasn't like the place was regularly patrolled, but there was a huge NO TRESPASSING sign posted by a "For Sale" sign. Both were old and battered, the ravages of time and weather catching up to them. Even Poppy Spencer hadn't been able to sell this white elephant.

Camp Miakoda might have sounded magical, especially if you knew that Miakoda meant "the power of the moon." But the harsh reality was this was an old boot camp for young offenders, and Levon had spent a summer here when he was seventeen, twenty-some years ago.

Camp Miakoda was a failed experiment, closed since the nineties, and the surrounding area was nothing but acres upon acres of crown land and conservation. The nearest residence was probably a cabin thirty miles away, maybe more.

Arabella squeezed her way through a hole in the barbed wire fence, careful not to snag her jeans on the jagged edges of the rusty hole someone had cut out years ago. She started down the path, nervous now, second-guessing her decision not to tell Emily where she was going. She had her phone in her back pocket but knew from past experience that there was no cell reception.

She wound her way along the path, stopping at a fork in the trail. Did she turn left or right? Her sense of direction was dismal at best and non-existent at worst. The last time she'd been here Levon had led the way, and she'd been scared witless. Arabella closed her eyes and tried to remember which way to go. She picked left and thought she recognized a small pond off in a clearing. Worst case, she'd probably end up back at the road instead of at the camp. At least she hoped that was the worst case.

The way into Camp Miakoda was a mix of overgrown shrubs, tree roots, and small rocks. The space felt claustrophobic, as if the road had tried to choke out any chance of survival. The mosquitoes got thicker and more insistent as dusk settled in. Arabella swatted them away ineffectively and wished she'd thought to douse herself with bug spray. After what seemed like hours, but was in fact less than forty-five minutes, she reached another fence, this one with a gatehouse and a gate, the kind where a button would be pushed by a gatekeeper to raise the arm up and let a vehicle go through. Twenty years ago the road to the gate would have been drivable, at least in the summer months, but years of neglect had changed all that.

Arabella slid underneath the wooden arm and made her way past a red brick building with small, leaded glass windows. With the exception of the odd curling shingle, the building still looked solid. She shivered despite the heat, thinking about the last time she'd been here.

A man was standing on the dock, surveying the river, his back to her. He was talking into something that looked like an old-fashioned cell phone, the kind with an antenna on the top.

The man was too tall for Levon. He was heavier too, even though he'd recently lost a lot of weight. But it wasn't his build or stature that gave him away. It was his uniform. The uniform of the Miakoda Falls Police Department. He put the phone in his pocket and pivoted to face her before Arabella had a chance to turn around and run the other way.

38

AARON BEECHAM GLARED AT ARABELLA, hands on his hips, his expression dark. "Whatever would bring you back to Camp Miakoda? Or should I rephrase that to say, who brought you back?"

Arabella swallowed hard. There was no sign of the compassionate man she'd dated. She considered playing the personal card and dismissed it. This was a cop doing a job, and any feelings he might still have for her had been compartmentalized—if he still had feelings for her. She decided to opt for complete transparency.

"Kerri St. Amour came by the Glass Dolphin a couple of hours ago. She wanted to gauge Emily's and my reaction to the murder of Trent Norland. She told us Levon was missing. She implied that you were looking for him. She also told me that you'd found an antique gun in the pond."

Aaron's eyes narrowed. "Kerri had no business telling you any of that. I specifically told her that I wanted to speak to you first."

"Kerri doesn't play by the rules. Everyone who knows her knows that. I'm surprised as a cop you haven't figured that out." She attempted a smile, but didn't quite succeed. "Or maybe you'd figured that out and didn't care as long as you got the media coverage you needed."

Beecham's face reddened, not quite a blush but getting there. She'd nailed it, then. They had been using Kerri, feeding her tidbits of information to get the whole meal. "You had to know that if you got in bed with a snake, you were bound to get bitten."

To Arabella's immense irritation, Beecham ignored the jab. Instead he asked her about Levon, and why she assumed he might be here.

"You know the answer to that as well as I do, Aaron. It all started here, for him." Except as soon as she said the words, she knew it wasn't true. It had all started for him the day Marc Larroquette left for a pack of smokes and never came back.

"He was here, earlier," Beecham said. "Or at least I assume it was him. There were footsteps in the sand by the dock that match his foot size. Size ten."

"Lots of men wear size ten," Arabella said, knowing full well those men probably had no connection to Camp Miakoda.

"Do they also have a penchant for denim? We found denim fibers on the fence."

"Denim is now an endangered fabric?"

"I hope Levon appreciates your loyalty." He pulled the oversized phone from his pocket, speaking into it in a low mumble before replacing it. "Constable Byrne has been searching the area by car."

"I didn't think there was cell reception here."

"There isn't. This is a walkie-talkie. Sometimes old school is the only school. Byrne is waiting by the fence. Come on, I'll walk you back before it gets dark."

"What if I'd like to take a look around first?"

"Trust me, Levon isn't here. I've searched the premises thoroughly, including the old hydro dam. I'm not sure why or when he came here, but he's gone now. Either that or he's hiding somewhere in the woods where no one can find him."

"What about inside the camp?"

"There's a padlock on the door. Even Levon isn't clever enough to enter a building and padlock the door behind him. I looked in the windows, dust on the floor and not a footstep to be found. No one's been in that building for years."

"What's going to happen to him if you find him?"

"Before he comes in voluntarily?"

"Yeah. Before that."

Beecham shrugged. "That will be Detective Merryfield's call. But it would be best if you stopped playing Nancy Drew. For your sake and Levon's."

Arabella bit back tears. The thought of losing Levon forever was too much to bear. "Did it occur to you that he might be in danger? He's not an idiot. He wouldn't toss his gun in the pond. He knows the pond gets dredged for golf balls, and he'd shown that gun to a few people, myself included. It would only be a matter of time until the police connected the gun to him."

Beecham's expression softened. "All we want to do is talk to him about the antique gun and his relationship with Trent Norland."

"The gun he might be able to help you with, but his relationship with Trent Norland? He didn't know him."

"That's what we need to find out. Just promise me you'll get him to come in to the station if he calls you."

"I'll personally drive him to the station."

After I call Isla Kempenfelt to meet us there.

Unless I kill him first for leading us all on a wild goose chase.

39

THEY WERE MAKING good time back to the road. Arabella didn't particularly enjoy hiking through the woods and as dusk settled in, she became grateful for Aaron's company. They fell into a companionable silence, and for a few minutes, she could almost imagine them being here under more pleasant circumstances.

Something changed at the midway point. Arabella glanced up at Aaron and was relieved to see that his expression hadn't altered. She kept her eyes on the path, in part to keep from tripping over tree roots, but mostly so she didn't give away her feelings. Because she absolutely knew Levon was following them. She could feel his eyes boring into her back.

She kept walking.

Relieved to be back to the road again, Arabella spotted Sarah Byrne right away, standing by the police car, waiting for them.

"Any luck?" Sarah asked.

Beecham shook his head. "Ms. Carpenter has promised to bring him into the station if he calls her."

Sarah raised her eyebrows. Arabella wasn't sure if it was because of the Ms. Carpenter reference or because of the promise extracted. Either way, it made her feel vulnerable. She wished that they would leave so Levon would come out of the woods. Maybe if she left first, and came back?

"I'm going to head into Lount's Landing and grab a late dinner."

"We're heading out as well," Beecham said. "We've spent enough time out here. It's time to get back to the station."

They got into their respective vehicles, Byrne driving the cop car, and Arabella following until they made the turn to Miakoda Falls. She stopped at the side of the road after she'd put a couple of miles behind her and took out her phone. If Beecham and Byrne came back to follow her she could pretend she needed to call Emily.

She waited fifteen minutes before she felt secure enough to turn back to Camp Miakoda. She drove by the entrance and continued along the County Road until she came to a small clearing in the woods. It was getting dark. She pulled a flashlight from her glove compartment, got out of the car, and started walking on the shoulder, looking behind herself every other step she took.

There was a rustling of leaves, and a shadowy figure emerged from the trees. Arabella jumped backwards, her heart pounding.

It was Levon, unshaven, dark circles under his eyes. *The scruffy look suits him*, Arabella thought, annoyed that such a thing had even crossed her mind. He was carrying a backpack.

"Where's your car?" she asked.

"I walked most of the way. Hitchhiked part of it."

"You walked here from your house?" It was miles away.

"Yeah. I brought some supplies and a blanket in my backpack. I'll admit it wasn't quite the adventure I was hoping for. I thought I'd be able to sleep in the main building. I'd forgotten about the padlock. And the mosquitos."

"You forgot a lot more than that. What on earth were you thinking?"

"All I knew was that I had to get away."

"How did you find out about Trent Norland?"

"Kerri St. Amour called me. She's a veritable wealth of information."

"She told me that you weren't answering your cell, that you'd up and disappeared."

"Disappeared might be a bit of an exaggeration. I just needed time to think. When I saw Beecham traipsing around here, I knew I was probably a suspect."

"Running away is going to convince them of your innocence?" Levon attempted a smile. "Admittedly, not one of my better ideas."

You can say that again. "Did Kerri mention the antique gun in the pond?"

"What?"

"Your antique gun. The Enfield? The police found it in the pond at the third hole of the Miakoda Falls Golf and Country Club."

"Surely they don't think I'd be that stupid. Why would I use a gun that could easily be traced back to me to kill two people?"

"The better question would be, how did your gun end up there if you didn't put it there? You always locked it up in a safe and stored the bullets separately, as required by law. At least you used to, when I lived there."

"I don't know."

"What don't you know?"

"I looked for it after my father was murdered, and it wasn't in the safe. I think it was stolen. But I didn't notice until after the murder. I could hardly go to the police and say, 'By the way, the murder weapon might be my antique gun, which I had locked up in a safe and now seems to be missing,' now could I?"

"Why not?"

"Because—" Levon shook his head, "I thought my father had taken it. He came by the house after our argument in the park. I didn't leave him alone for long, but I had a call I didn't want him to hear, so I went outside. He could have taken it then."

"But it was locked in the safe."

"I'm terrible at remembering numbers. You know that. I had a label at the back of the safe with the combination written on it. He would have remembered that I did that with every combination lock I owned."

Levon was terrible about remembering numbers: phone numbers, postal codes, addresses. He was hopeless. But putting a label with the combination on the back of a safe? Even if Marc had taken the gun, he hadn't shot himself, and he certainly hadn't shot Trent Norland.

"We need to call Isla Kempenfelt and fill her in. Then we need to go to the police station and you have to tell them everything." There was no need to tell him about her promise to Aaron Beecham.

"I'm not looking forward to it, but you're right." Levon rubbed a hand against his jaw. "Do you mind if I clean up before we go to the station? I haven't had a shower or a shave for forty-eight hours."

Arabella knew they should get there sooner rather than later, but a clean-shaven Levon would be more believable than the vagrant version standing before her. And Beecham did say that all they wanted to do was talk to Levon. He wasn't an actual suspect—yet.

"Fine. We'll stop at your house on the way. But don't screw me over on this, Levon. If you do, I'll never forgive you."

"I promise. Believe me, I just want this nightmare to be over with."

So did Arabella, but she had a feeling the nightmare was just beginning.

40

THE NIGHTMARE STARTED AS SOON as they were back in the car. "Trent called me three days ago," Levon said while Arabella drove. "He claimed to have information about my father that I should know about."

"And so you arranged to meet him on the walking trail behind the golf course?"

"No. I was supposed to meet him at the Miakoda Falls Golf and Country Club, in the clubhouse restaurant, at noon. I went there and waited for him, but he never showed up."

"Maybe he changed his mind about talking to you."

"That's what I thought. Now I figure he was already dead. Anyway, when I got back to the golf course parking lot, Luke was standing outside the clubhouse, talking to Gilly and Robbie Andrews, the head pro. They were in a deep discussion, but I wasn't close enough to hear and I didn't want to draw attention to myself. I got in my car and hightailed it out of there."

"Could they have seen you?"

"Yes. Even if they hadn't, the waitress definitely saw me, so the police will be able to trace me to the area."

Arabella bit her lip. "What about Luke? Was he dressed for golf?"

"Now that you mention it, no. But he could have been there for any number of reasons. I know he's good friends with Robbie."

The question was, who had called Trent? Because, whoever it was, they'd obviously asked to meet him on the trail by the third hole. Maybe they had pretended to be Levon. But then they would have known the two were planning to meet. Arabella was still mulling over the possibilities when she pulled into Levon's driveway. She'd been half expecting to find the police waiting at his house, and was relieved to find no sign of them.

"We're here. Time to clean up. I'll call Isla Kempenfelt while you shower, shave, and change."

Levon nodded and got out of the car. Arabella followed him into the house, blushing slightly at the memory of her last visit. There would be no repeating that, not today and not ever again. They were friends; strictly platonic. Arabella called Kempenfelt's emergency number while Levon headed into the shower. She told the night receptionist it really was an emergency situation and was transferred promptly, no questions asked. A brief recap of the events was enough for the lawyer to agree to meet them at the Miakoda Falls Police Station within the hour.

"I'll let Detective Merryfield know we're coming," Kempenfelt said, before hanging up.

Levon was quick to clean up, his hair slightly damp, his clothes changed, dirty denim for fresh.

Arabella filled him in on her conversation with the lawyer. "Thank you...for everything."

"I haven't done anything you wouldn't have done for me," Arabella said.

They were halfway to Miakoda Falls when she spotted a white Honda CRV behind them. "Damn it," Arabella said. Maybe if she'd taken the direct route, she wouldn't even have noticed the car following them. The graveled back road leading into town was usually only used by local residents. It was a dark and almost moonless night, but the license plate was lit. Arabella knew who it belonged to. It could only spell one thing: trouble.

"Kerri St. Amour is following us," Arabella said, instinctively speeding up.

Levon turned around. "What? Pull over. I don't want a confrontation outside the cop shop. I can just imagine the headlines."

Pulling over was the last thing Arabella wanted to do, but Levon had a point. She turned on her indicator signal, slowed down, and made her way onto the shoulder of the road. Kerri slid in behind her and hopped out of the car, phone in hand.

"Stay here," Arabella said, too late. Levon was already out of the car.

"Ditch the phone, Kerri," Levon said. "I'm not interested in taking a selfie with either one of you, and I'm definitely not interested in seeing my face splashed on the front page."

To Arabella's surprise, Kerri put the phone away.

"How long have you been following me?" Levon asked.

"I've been waiting outside of your house for hours. I knew you'd be home eventually."

"I didn't notice your car," Arabella said.

"Please, that's for amateurs," Kerri said, rolling her eyes. "I parked down the street and waited inside Levon's garage."

"So you were trespassing," Levon said.

Kerri shrugged. "Prove it. I'm not there now. In case you weren't aware, the police have been looking for you."

"I'm aware." Levon kicked a stone and watched it trickle into the ditch. "We're on our way to the station in Miakoda Falls now. I'd appreciate it if you didn't follow us."

"What's in it for me if I don't?"

Not getting a black eye, Arabella thought.

Levon smiled and turned on the charm. "I promise to give you first dibs on what might be an exclusive story."

"So you admit there is a story." Kerri smirked. "I'm thinking it would be breaking news to see you enter the police station in the dark of night."

"Half the town can see the very well-lit police station. It will be no secret I'm going in to speak with the police. That's hardly an exclusive story."

"How do I know that I can trust you?"

"You don't. Come on, Arabella. We're running late." Levon turned away from Kerri and marched back to the car.

Arabella started to follow him, then stopped and walked back. "He's a good man, Kerri. Don't screw him over. If Levon says he'll give you first dibs on his story, he will."

Kerri pressed her lips together. "I want your story, too—yours and Emily's."

"Everyone knows our story. It was front-page news not long ago," Arabella said, deliberately misunderstanding Kerri. "But we can talk later."

Like in ten years.

41

ISLA KEMPENFELT WAS WAITING for them at the Miakoda Falls Police Station. Once again, Isla's fine- boned features struck Arabella; she looked more like a ballerina than a criminal lawyer. Maybe that was part of her success. You didn't expect a pit bull in a whippet's body.

"You'll have to wait here, Arabella," Kempenfelt said, pointing to an uncomfortable looking bench.

The thought of sitting there waiting for Levon was unappealing. "I can leave and come back when Levon's ready. It's only a thirty-minute drive from Lount's Landing."

"I don't think Officer Beecham will approve. He asked me to let him know when you arrived.

Detective Merryfield will be questioning Levon."

Arabella was trying to figure a way out when Aaron entered the lobby. She followed him without a word, knowing it was pointless to argue.

The interview room wasn't much bigger than a broom closet.

"I'm going to be taping our conversation," Beecham said. "Do you want to have a lawyer present?

I'm afraid Ms. Kempenfelt is otherwise engaged."

"Do I need a lawyer?"

Beecham smiled. "Only you know the answer to that. But you can stop the interview at any time and ask for one."

"Then I'll pass. For now."

Beecham nodded and started the tape recorder. After setting up the time, date, and other particulars, he started. "The last time I saw you, you were driving back to Lount's Landing. Where did you find Levon?"

"I saw him walking along the road." Arabella crossed her fingers underneath the table, hoping Beecham wouldn't ask which road.

No such luck. "Which road?"

Arabella sighed. She wasn't cut out for this. A lifetime of telling it as it was didn't prepare her for fabricating a story. She just hoped Levon told Merryfield the same story.

They hadn't discussed it, which, in retrospect, was stupid. Then again, Levon knew her. He knew she would have to tell the truth.

Wouldn't he?

"I knew, instinctively, that Levon was at the camp."

"So you saw him when I was with you and didn't say anything."

"No, I didn't see him. But I knew he was there. Levon and I were married, we have a connection." Time to fabricate, just a bit. "I tried to ignore the feeling, and I started back home. But by the time I got to the turn-off for Lount's Landing, I'd second- and third-guessed myself and had to turn back. And so I did." She filled Beecham in on the rest.

"So Levon's story is that he had an appointment to meet with Trent Norland. When he didn't show, he left. Does that about sum it up?"

"Perfectly."

"What about his gun?"

"He said it had gone missing. He didn't notice until after Marc Larroquette was found dead."

"How convenient."

"It's far from convenient. If he'd discovered the gun missing earlier, he would have reported it. As it was, he knew you'd suspect him. When Kerri told him about Trent Norland's death, his instinct was to run. It was a shortsighted, poor decision on his part, but he's innocent."

Sarah Byrne popped her head into the room and gestured to Beecham. He followed her out into the hallway. He was back within a couple of minutes.

"Interview with Arabella Carpenter concluded." Beecham turned off the tape recorder. "You're free to go."

"I'm free to go?" What had Byrne told Beecham?

"Unless you want to spend more quality time with me. That can be arranged."

Arabella took the hint and had barely made it to the lobby when Levon joined her. The dark circles under his eyes were still there, but there was a spring to his step that hadn't been there earlier.

"Where's Isla Kempenfelt?" Arabella asked.

"She's chatting with Merryfield and I don't think it's entirely about police business," Levon said.

He pushed open the door. "Let's get out of here before they change their mind about letting me go."

Arabella peppered Levon with questions on the way to his house. Did he tell the same story as she had? Why did he think they let him go? Did they think he was innocent?

He'd told them about the missing gun, about arranging to meet Trent and getting stood up. He'd just gotten to the part about Gilly, Robbie, and Luke in the parking lot when Sarah Byrne had come in. Merryfield had gone out in the hall to talk to her. When he came back, he thanked Levon and Kempenfelt for their time and stopped the interview.

"The same thing happened to me," Arabella said, pulling into Levon's driveway. "Whatever Byrne told them must have cleared you of any wrongdoing."

"Let's hope it stays that way."

Arabella grinned. "There is an even brighter side."

"Which is?"

"You don't have much of a story to tell Kerri."

"Yeah. I feel terrible about that." Levon laughed, and then Arabella started laughing too, the tension of the past two days melting away. Before she knew it, they were heading into his house, and he was pouring them each a cognac.

"I really shouldn't," Arabella said, taking a sip and feeling the liquid warm her belly. "I'm driving."

"I'll make you some coffee and a snack before you go. I even have shortbread." He would.

"I'm trying to give up cookies, and coffee will keep me up. Plus I really need to sleep. I'm exhausted."

"Then finish your cognac and stay here."

"I thought we agreed—"

"We did. I meant in the spare bedroom."

Arabella felt an irrational surge of disappointment. She held out her brandy snifter, the amber liquid already drained. "One more and then I really need to get some sleep. In the spare bedroom."

It was three o'clock in the morning when Arabella woke up. Just like the last time she'd stayed over, her head was pounding and her mouth felt as though it was filled with cotton batten.

At least she was in the spare bedroom. There was just one problem.

Levon was lying there next to her, the duvet tucked under his chin, his breathing slow and easy, his hair falling softly over his eyes. She pulled the pillow out from under her head, placed it over her head, and let out a silent scream.

Damn cognac did it every single time.

42

Arabella was showered and dressed by six a.m., an ungodly hour, but she wanted to get home, change, and get to the Glass Dolphin before Emily arrived. The last thing she wanted to do was discuss the previous evening's events with Emily, and straggling in late was sure to start up a conversation. She rummaged through the cupboards, found a stainless steel travel mug, popped a coffee pod into Levon's one-cup coffeemaker, and pressed the button, comforted by the gurgling sound. His pantry cupboard revealed a box of quinoa oatmeal granola bars—whoever thought that combination was a good idea had some serious rethinking to do—unsalted soda crackers, a box of no-name bran flakes, and two tins of chicken noodle soup.

The refrigerator's contents were equally dire: milk that didn't quite pass the sniff test, a small bar of corner-hardened white cheese, which might have been cheddar or mozzarella in a past life, and a couple of Granny Smith apples. The thought of a sour apple on top of last night's cognac turned her stomach, but no more than the thought of a sickly sweet granola bar. She reopened the pantry door and grabbed a handful of soda crackers. It would have to do until she could get a proper breakfast at the Sunrise Café. She grabbed the mug and was just about out the door when Levon sauntered into the kitchen.

"You were going to leave without saying good-bye." It was a statement, not a question. "You're starting to make a habit out of that. I'm starting to take it personally."

"I need to get home and change before I go to the shop."

"So it's not personal?"

Arabella shook her head. "No. Yes. We can't go down this road again, Levon. It always ends up badly."

"Maybe this time will be different."

"I don't have time to debate this right now."

"How about dinner tonight? We can meet at The Hanged Man's Noose. You'll be perfectly safe there. I won't even let Betsy serve you cognac. A glass of chardonnay is the strongest you'll get. I know you love her Full Noose Nachos."

It was a tempting offer. She was just about to say yes when the sound of the front door opening stopped her. Who had a key? Arabella glanced at Levon and watched as the color drained from his face.

"That will be Gilly Germaine," Levon said. "She has a key. How convenient."

"It's not what you think."

"It never is with you, Levon. It never is." Arabella slammed the travel mug onto the counter and stormed out of the room. A surprised looking Gilly was hanging up her jacket on the coat rack.

"Arabella?"

"In the flesh. And in case you were wondering, it's exactly what it seems."

Y

BY THE TIME Arabella arrived at the Sunrise Café she was almost calm, almost being the operative word. A long, hot shower had helped, as had two ibuprofen and three antacid tablets. But she was still mad, more at herself than at Levon. He hadn't promised her a damn thing, hadn't led her astray, unless you counted the cognac, and she was her own liquor control board, as that old LCBO liquor store ad had said.

The restaurant was almost full, with Fran bustling from one table to the other, pouring coffee and taking orders. Arabella thought the chatter had quieted when she took a seat, but she shook off the feeling. The morning's events had left her feeling raw and exposed.

"What'll it be, hon?" Fran smiled. "Let me guess. Cinnamon raisin bagel with peanut butter, and coffee, black and strong. To go."

"Coffee, black and strong, in a mug, the biggest one you've got. Two eggs over easy, home fries, rye toast, light on the butter, and bacon, well done. To stay."

Fran grinned. "Does someone have another hangover?"

"Guilty as charged."

"I'll be right back. I know an emergency situation when I see one."

Y

ARABELLA FINISHED her coffee and the last of her breakfast.

"You want some coffee in a to-go cup?" Fran placed the check on the table. "Yeah, that would be great, thank you."

"I guess you two were celebrating last night. You and Levon."

"Celebrating?"

"I thought you knew. Levon is officially in the clear. The police have another suspect in the Trent Norland murder. They brought the guy in late last night."

That would explain the quick exit from the police station but... "How do you know?"

"Kerri's blog, of course, even if she won't admit to writing it. It's all anyone can talk about. Of course, there's no evidence the same person killed Levon's dad, but this Kerri—I mean, 'this blogger'— seems to think it's a given."

"How did Kerri find out?"

Fran shrugged. "Who knows? She seems to have eyes and ears

everywhere. Anyway, I know you and Levon have remained friends. So I figured you were celebrating."

Was there an emphasis on the word "friends?" Arabella would have loved to dwell on that thought a little while longer, but the latest news gave her a momentary sense of relief: she knew Levon wasn't guilty. Then who was?

"Who did the police arrest?"

"The owner of that marina in Lakeside. Luke Surmanski."

The greasy breakfast roiled in her stomach and Arabella wished she'd stuck with her usual dry toast. First Kevin, then Johnny Porter, and now Luke. When it came to men, Emily sure could pick them.

43

Arabella was busy sorting through the boxes of inventory they'd purchased from Heidi—there was plenty they could list on eBay for what she hoped would be a relatively quick turnaround for some much-needed cash—when Emily blew into the Glass Dolphin. She was out of breath and her usually flawless complexion was red and blotchy.

"Oh. My. God," Emily said. "We have to do something. You will not believe who's being questioned in the murder of Trent Norland."

"Luke Surmanski."

"Yes, but how on earth did you find out?"

Arabella filled Emily in on her breakfast at the Sunrise Café.

"Damn, that Kerri St. Amour is good," Emily said, temporarily sidetracked, and with grudging admiration. "How did she find out?"

"Fran said Kerri has 'eyes and ears everywhere,' whatever that means. The bigger question would be, how did you find out?"

"Hudson called me late last night. He tried to reach you, but you weren't answering." Was there an accusation there? If so, Arabella chose to ignore it.

"What did he say?"

"That it has to be a big misunderstanding."

Arabella wasn't so sure. After all, Luke had lied to the police about recognizing Marc Larroquette, and renting a houseboat with the only source of ID a pleasure craft operator's card seemed a bit loosey-goosey for someone who ran a successful marina. What if he'd lied about other things?

"Does Hudson know what evidence the police have on Luke?"

"I don't know. He said whatever they have, it must be circumstantial." Emily bit her lip. "I just know that Luke is innocent. I've gotten to know him, and—don't give me that look, Arabella."

"What look?"

"That look that says when it comes to men, my judgment is sorely lacking. I'm telling you, Luke is different."

"I believe you."

"No, you don't. I'm sure you're relieved that Levon's off the hook for the Trent Norland murder, at least, but now Luke needs our help, as in you and me and Hudson."

"What do you mean, 'Levon's off the hook, at least for the Trent Norland murder?'"

"There's still the question of Marc Larroquette's death."

"Surely you don't believe..." Arabella leveled Emily with her best how-dare-you stare. "Of course not, but I also don't believe Luke is guilty. Do you?"

"I don't know. I know you're into him, but how well do we really know Luke? It's possible that he drove to the third hole, killed Marc, and went back to the clubhouse to ride back out to the course with us. He said that he was going to check on the jet ski, but we only have his word for it."

"We also have Hudson's word."

"For all we know, Hudson could be an accomplice. He said he was going to the silent auction table. Maybe he was acting as a lookout."

"A lookout? Listen to yourself."

"I'm just trying to help."

"That's your idea of helping Luke? Implicating Hudson? I thought you liked him."

"We're trying to sort out whether Luke could be innocent. I'm not sure what else you want from me."

"I want you to meet Hudson for lunch at the Noose today at noon. He asked us to join him to discuss theories. He thought three heads would be better than one."

"What about the store?"

"I've already called Caitie. She's more than happy to help out."

"It sounds like you have everything worked out." Arabella knew she sounded cranky, but she was tired of playing detective. She was also tired of men: Levon, Hudson, Luke. They were all a pain in the ass.

"Will you come with me?"

Arabella sighed. Sometimes the price of partnership came high. "Yes, I'll come with you."

"Thank you," Emily said as she picked up one of the boxes of Cornflower glass that Arabella had just sorted and labeled with "eBay." She took it to her computer desk at the back of the shop. "I'll get started on listing these straight away. Staying busy will keep my mind off Luke until it's time to leave. And Arabella?"

"Yes?"

"Stop sleeping with Levon. It's messing with your chi."

"I'm not—"

"Oh please. I stopped off at the Sunrise Café on the way here. I thought I might pick up some nugget of gossip that could help Luke. Fran mentioned that you'd been in and had bacon and eggs."

Sometimes this town was too small to be believed. "So I had bacon and eggs. From that you determined I slept with Levon?"

"You left here on a mission yesterday afternoon. I figured you were off looking for Levon, and it turned out I was right. According to Kerri's blog, you and Levon went to the police station last night. Levon is no longer a suspect. You celebrated. When you're hungover you eat dry toast or grease like bacon and eggs. And the only thing that gives you a serious hangover is cognac. Levon, cognac—I did the math. When are the two of you going to admit you're still stuck on each other?"

Arabella wasn't about to mention Gilly's surprise visit. "Is there anything else you want to lecture me about? Or can we try to get some work done?"

"I would appreciate it if you gave Luke the same benefit of the doubt that I extended to Levon." Arabella nodded. "I can do that."

Or at least try.

Another smile. "All we have to figure out is what the police have on him and then find a way to disprove it. Without implicating Levon again, of course."

"Is that all?" Arabella said. "That's all."

It was the way she twitched her shoulders that gave her away. There was more to this story than Emily was telling her. How much more remained to be seen.

44

THE HANGED MAN'S Noose was doing decent business for a weekday morning. Betsy greeted Arabella and Emily at the door. "Hudson's already here," she said, leading the way. "Nina's all about comfort food today. The specials are mac and cheese or veggie lasagna. Hudson's going with the mac and cheese."

Nina was a great cook, but the thought of either made Arabella's stomach churn. She took a seat across from Hudson.

"The veggie lasagna sounds great," Emily said, sitting next to Arabella. "Anything to drink?"

"White wine spritzer with lime and lots of ice."

"Coors Light," Hudson said.

"Bottle or glass?"

"Glass."

"Arabella?"

"Just club soda for me," Arabella replied, catching Betsy's look out of the corner of her eye. It was the one that said, we've been friends forever and the only time you order just a club soda is when you're hungover. She hated that she felt the need to explain. "I had a big breakfast. I didn't realize I was coming here for lunch."

Betsy grinned. "Uh-huh. One club soda coming right up." As soon as Betsy left, Hudson got right to the point.

"Here's what I know. Detective Merryfield has interviewed me three times. Each time he asked the same questions. Did I know Marc Larroquette? Answer: no. Did I know Trent Norland? Answer: not before the day of the golf tournament. Did I belong to or know of an organization called 'fist?'" Hudson closed his hand to demonstrate.

Arabella glanced at Emily. She hadn't told her about the connection to FYSST.

"Fist?" Arabella said, mimicking Hudson's closed hand. She needed to know what he knew.

"Yes, fist," Hudson said. "And once again, the answer was no. Luke told me they asked him the same questions."

"And his answers were also no?"

Hudson took a moment to reply. "Yeah…but…on the day of the golf tournament, Luke told the police that he didn't recognize the body. Later, he admitted he did, but couldn't place him because the man he'd met had been wearing a baseball cap and sunglasses."

"That's plausible," Emily said. "I've run into people that I know from swimming or golf, and I can't place them out of context."

"Except that Marc Larroquette rented a houseboat from Luke using only a Pleasure Craft Operator ID card."

"With Kevin Hollister Cartwright's name on it," Emily said. "Luke said Marc paid cash, including a damage deposit."

Hudson frowned. "Even so, houseboats aren't inexpensive. What if he'd totaled it, or, had stolen it? What would he say to his insurance company? The more I think about it, the less likely I believe that Luke would rent to a stranger without a credit card or driver's license for back up. I didn't question it at the time, but you can be sure the police have."

Arabella had been thinking the same thing. There was also the "coincidence" of Marc renting the houseboat under the name of Kevin Hollister Cartwright, Emily's ex-fiancé.

"Are you suggesting that Luke knew Marc Larroquette?" Emily asked.

Hudson shook his head. "No, but I do think he knew Kevin Hollister Cartwright. He didn't know 'Kevin' was really Marc Larroquette."

Everyone leaned back in their seats and thought. Arabella put together what she knew. Chloe was Marc's stepdaughter. Chloe had lived with Kevin after Kevin had broken up with Emily. It was possible that Chloe had told Marc about Emily Garland, Kevin's ex. Maybe Chloe told him Emily had moved to Lount's Landing and owned part of an antiques shop. It wouldn't take long for Marc to find out that Arabella Carpenter had founded the store.

If Marc Larroquette had been keeping tabs on Levon—and Arabella was sure he had—then he'd know that she had once been married to his son.

She told the others what she was thinking, concluding with, "What I don't know is why Marc felt the need to drag Emily into this, and he had to know using the name of her ex-fiancé would do just that—unless he was trying to send a message. I'm not sure what message he was trying to send or to whom. It's bizarre."

Hudson nodded. "It also doesn't explain how Luke knew Marc Larroquette, regardless of what name he was using."

"Does Luke have a tattoo?" Arabella asked.

"He doesn't have any tattoos," Emily said, and blushed.

Hudson looked confused. "What does having a tattoo have to do with this?"

Betsy came by with their drinks and slid into the empty seat next to Hudson. "Finally, a break in the action. So who's getting a tattoo? Are you finally going to get a tat, Arabella?"

Betsy had a tattoo of a pink butterfly at the nape of her neck. You didn't see it unless she wore her hair up, unlike the small noose on the inside of her right wrist. That one she liked to show off whenever she could.

"The only thing I might consider as a permanent addition to my body would be diamond stud earrings," Arabella said with a smile.

"I already have the Canadian flag on my ankle," said Emily. "It's the only body art I need."

"Then it must be you, Hudson." Betsy said.

He shook his head. "Like Arabella, I'm a holdout when it comes to tattoos. We were talking about Luke Surmanski."

"Then I'm with Hudson," Betsy said. "Why does it matter if Luke has a tattoo?"

"That's what I was trying to find out," Hudson said.

"Not just a tattoo," Arabella said. "A specific tattoo of a wagon wheel with the letters F-Y-S-S-T around each spoke."

"F-Y-S-S-T," Hudson said. "Not F-I-S-T."

"Exactly. It stands for Face Yesterday, Save Someone Tomorrow. It was started by a couple of men who wanted to do something good. What we do know is that Marc Larroquette was a member. He even headed up a branch, if you can call it that, in Northern Ontario. If Luke had the tattoo, it meant he, too, was a member."

"That doesn't mean he wasn't a member," Betsy said. "It just means he didn't get the tattoo." Emily picked at her napkin and started shredding it into strips. "Luke has an aversion to needles."

"So not having the tattoo…" Betsy said.

"Doesn't mean he wasn't a member," Emily said, and started to cry.

45

BY UNSPOKEN AGREEMENT, there was no more talk about Luke until they'd finished eating. Arabella regretted her earlier decision not to order anything, but Betsy had her covered with a mini order of Full Noose Nachos.

"On the house," Betsy said with a wink, sliding the plate on the table.

Food eaten, dishes cleared, and drinks replenished, it was time to address the subject of Luke once again. Emily started the conversation. "I think it's safe to assume that Luke knew Marc Larroquette. I also think it's safe to assume the police have come to the same conclusion."

Hudson nodded. "I agree. Anything else?"

"I think FYSST is the most obvious connection," Emily said, "but I'm inclined to believe that he knew Marc as Kevin Hollister Cartwright, which would explain the houseboat rental."

"I hate to ask," Arabella said, "but did you and Luke ever talk about Kevin?"

Emily shook her head. "I told him that before I moved to Lount's Landing, I'd been serious with a guy in Toronto, but I wouldn't have mentioned his name. In fact, if the guy I'm dating name-drops, it's a red flag to me that they're still hung up on their ex. I figure the reverse is true. So, yeah, Luke would have known there used to be a guy in Toronto, but not his name."

"The next obvious question, why would Luke want to join an organization like FYSST?" Arabella asked.

Emily shook her head. "I don't really know much about his past, outside of what he's told me. His mom and dad live in Toronto. He gets along with them, and they have dinner together on the last Sunday of every month. He has an older sister who lives in Alberta. He hasn't seen her in a couple of years, but they text each other on a regular basis."

"That's what he told me, too. But I'll bet that's not the story Kerri St. Amour is planning to write," Hudson said.

"And you know this, how?" Emily asked.

"Because I had the 'pleasure' of speaking to her early this morning," Hudson said, using air quotes around the word pleasure. "She grilled me about Luke's past, and intimated that there were some buried secrets. I wasn't sure if Kerri was trying to get me to tell her things she didn't know, or if she knew things that I don't."

"What did you tell her?" Emily asked.

"Exactly what you just told us, but I haven't known Luke all that long. We met when I moved to Lakeside."

Arabella wondered if Luke had a secret he was willing to kill two men for. "You need to call Chloe," Arabella said to Emily.

"Who's Chloe?" Hudson asked.

Arabella filled him in while Emily stared at her hands.

"Arabella's right," Hudson said. "Chloe may have some answers."

Emily nodded. "I know. I've been putting it off, hoping it wouldn't be necessary. I'll call her as soon as we get back to the shop. I can't promise she'll want to speak to me, though."

"All you can do is try," Arabella said, but a big part of her was worried about the outcome. What if Chloe's answers hurt Luke, instead of helped him? What if Kerri St. Amour had been there before her?

What if Luke really was guilty?

46

WHEN EMILY MADE the call she was surprised that Chloe not only agreed to meet with her, but also offered to make the trip to Lount's Landing the next day.

"She's going to come here? To the Glass Dolphin?" Arabella asked. "She said she needed to get out of Toronto for a day."

"Hmm. Well, if you've got the store covered, I'm going to see Levon."

Emily didn't push it. She had enough on her mind without worrying about Arabella's love life. "Safe travels, then."

Emily had a hard time concentrating while she waited for Chloe, but she managed to list a handful of items on eBay and check on the status of a dozen more, in between helping the occasional person who wandered into the store. She was wrapping a pink Depression glass platter for a customer when the door chimed. It was Chloe. She'd ditched her usual spandex for a floral skirt, white tee shirt, and sandals; her blonde hair was pulled back in a ponytail. She wore minimal makeup though her red- rimmed eyes had been heavily mascaraed. Chloe had been crying, and crying hard.

Chloe waited until the customer left the shop before speaking. When she did, the words tumbled out in a rush. "Kevin's left me, and it's all because of that bastard Marc Laurentian. Or should I say Larroquette. God, he didn't even use his real name when he married my mother. She always did know how to pick a loser."

"I'm sorry. I know firsthand how much it hurts to get dumped." It wasn't meant to be a dig. Kevin left her for Chloe, but kicking someone when they were down wasn't her style.

"Yeah. I guess you do, thanks to me."

"I used to blame you, but I came to realize our breakup wasn't your fault. Kevin likes to get engaged, but he's not the marrying kind. As you've just found out."

"It's true we've been arguing lately, mostly about money. He thought we were spending too much on the wedding."

"If that's the case, why did you blame Marc Laurentian?"

"Because he came to town spouting who-knows-what sort of nonsense. Kevin was livid. He considers organized religion a cult. Something like FYSST sent him over the edge. And then Marc used Kevin's name to rent that houseboat. He went ballistic over that."

"Kevin told me he thought Marc asked you for a donation to the cause. Did he?"

The two red splotches on Chloe's face told all. "Yes, but I didn't tell Kevin about it. He was already angry enough. Besides it was more like blackmail than a request for a donation."

"Blackmail?"

Chloe nodded. "I got pregnant at sixteen and gave the baby up for adoption. A boy. I didn't want to, but my home life was hardly conducive to bringing in a baby."

"Did Kevin know?"

"I planned to tell him, and then time went on and it was like, now I can't tell him, because he'll think I've been lying to him all this time."

Not telling wasn't exactly a lie, but Emily knew that Kevin would have seen it that way. He lived in a very black-and-white world.

"Did Marc threaten to tell Kevin about the baby if you didn't give him money? That hardly sounds like a guy trying to make amends."

"The only amends Marc Laurentian would make would be the ones that directly benefited him.

The man was pond scum."

Pond scum was an interesting choice of words, given where the gun was found. "Do you think Marc knew Kevin? Before coming to see you, I mean?"

"I'm positive they never met. To say Marc and I weren't close would be an understatement. The day I left home was the happiest day of my life."

"What about Luke Surmanski?"

"I don't know if Marc knew Luke, but I'm sure Kevin didn't know him. He would have told me."

"So you don't think Marc was trying to send a message, renting the houseboat in Kevin's name?"

"A message? No. It was just the sort of sadistic game that Marc would play to mess with my head.

He always was an asshole." She wiped away a tear. "I'm sorry. I came here looking for answers. It looks like you don't have any for me. At least none that I want to hear."

Y

LONG AFTER CHLOE left and the shop had closed for the night, Emily sat in the store as if Chloe's answers might come to her.

They didn't.

Y

ARABELLA ARRIVED at Levon's without calling him first, and was thankful to find him alone. She wasn't sure what she would have done if Gilly had been there.

He answered the door, barefoot and bare-chested, his jeans skimming the wood floor. The man wasn't playing fair.

"Arabella. I wasn't expecting you. Not after…" He let the sentence hang.

"Not after Gilly came in with a key," she finished for him. "That's why I'm here."

"Because Gilly has a key? I mean, she had a key, when we were dating, but she gave it back. At least, I thought she had. Maybe I asked for it back and didn't follow up. Or maybe she made a copy. The point is—"

"The point is Gilly has a key, which means she had access to your safe. And your gun." Levon blanched, then nodded. "Why didn't I think of that?"

"You might have, eventually, at least if you started thinking with your head instead of with your hormones. Did she know where to find the combination?"

"Yes. I showed her the gun when she was telling me about using an authentic shotgun start. She was fascinated by the history."

"I'm sure she was. Did she see you open the safe?"

"Yes, now that you mention it. She would have noticed me checking the back of the safe for the label."

"That's something you need to tell Merryfield."

"You don't think Gilly killed—"

"I don't know what to think. Maybe she stole the gun and gave it to the killer. Maybe she's the killer. All I know is Luke Surmanski is in jail right now under suspicion of murder. Maybe he's innocent or maybe he isn't, but the police should have all the facts."

Levon sighed. "I suppose you're right. I just don't have to like it."

47

ARABELLA OPENED the door to the Glass Dolphin and was surprised to find Emily sitting in the same clothes she'd worn the day before.

"Whoa. You look bad. Were you here all night?"

"Yes."

"What on earth did Chloe tell you?"

Emily filled her in, making sure not to leave anything out, including her own unwelcome conclusion.

"Let me get this straight. You believe that Marc Larroquette had something on Luke, and that's the reason Luke rented him the houseboat without proper ID and a credit card?"

"I don't want to believe it, but I've already called Hudson to run the idea by him. He can't imagine what Marc could blackmail Luke over. Then again, he hasn't known him that long either. We both took what he told us about himself at face value. I feel so stupid."

"First of all, it's conjecture on your part. Second of all, we all have things we'd rather not have people know about."

"Blackmail-able things?"

Arabella thought about her life so far. There were a few things she'd rather not tell the world, but nothing she'd pay money to stop from getting out. "I don't know."

"What about your recent evenings with Levon? Anything worth blackmailing you over?" It was a pathetic attempt at humor, but at least Emily was trying.

"I'm afraid I feel every bit as stupid as you. I did spend the night at Levon's house, twice. I blamed it on cognac, but if I'm being honest, a part of me thought we might be able to get past the past."

"And did you?"

Arabella sighed. "No. You'd think I'd have learned by now. Of course, Levon denies it, but I'm sure he is—or was—still seeing Gilly Germaine, even though they've supposedly broken up. As a matter of fact, when I called him a few days ago to see how he was holding up, I heard Gilly's voice in the background."

"She might have stopped by for another reason."

"That's what I tried to tell myself. But a couple of days ago, I was getting ready to leave when Gilly opened the front door. With a key. Levon said, 'It's not what it seems,' to me, meaning Gilly having a key wasn't what it seemed. And I looked at Gilly and said, 'In case you were wondering, it's exactly what it seems.'"

Emily laughed. "I would have loved to see the expression on her face. But if you're so ticked off with Levon, why did you go there yesterday?"

"Because if Gilly had a key, she could have been the one to take the gun from his safe."

"And you couldn't tell him on the phone?"

"I wanted to see the expression on his face." She wasn't about to admit, not even to herself, that part of her wanted to see him again. "He promised to call Merryfield and tell him, not that he was happy about it. He doesn't believe Gilly shot Marc or Trent."

"And you do?"

"Not really. But she might have stolen the gun for whoever did."

"That would make her an accomplice, but it doesn't make Luke look any less guilty. Luke could have been the one she stole the gun for. Any other theories?"

"Levon admitted Gilly was fascinated by the history of the gun, the connection to the British military, and the North-West Mounted

Police. Maybe she stole it because she loves guns. She did insist on using a real shotgun at the tournament, after all."

"And then someone stole the gun from her, shot two men, and tossed it in the pond. That's a lot of gun stealing."

"I know it's a stretch."

"Ya think?" Emily flushed. "I'm sorry, that came across wrong. I didn't sleep much last night."

Arabella looked at her friend with concern. "You really do look dreadful. Go home and get some rest. I'll look after the shop today. I promise to call you if anything comes up."

Y

EMILY MEANT TO GO HOME, but her stomach grumbled, and she realized that her last meal had been lunch the day before. She decided to grab breakfast at the Sunrise Café. Coffee and an order of French toast with maple syrup would go down nicely. Against her better judgment, she picked up the latest issue of *Inside the Landing* from the newspaper box outside the diner.

Kerri St. Amour's report about the murder of Trent Norland and Luke's arrest ran under the headline ANTIQUE GUN FOUND IN POND. It filled the front page and continued on page three, where head shots of Luke and Trent dominated. She had even managed to find a photo of Luke that made him look like a criminal, whereas Trent's looked like the sort of professional shot you'd find on a business website.

Fran brought her a coffee. "I only had time to read the headlines. Fill me in on the details. And don't forget to check out her blog. Might as well get all the gossip."

She's outdone herself this time, Emily thought, leaving the paper open on the table and pulling up

Outside the Landing on her phone to read the latest entry, posted just this morning.

A HOLE IN TWO!

Golfers will tell you that a hole in one is a rare occurrence, as is a
single murder in our little town. But we now have a hole in two.
Marc Larroquette scored A DEADLY BULLET hole in his chest
at the Miakoda Falls Golf and Country Club. Yesterday Trent
Norland was shot and killed, his body found by a dog walker on the
trail behind the third hole of the golf course.
Levon Larroquette, the estranged son of Marc, was originally
suspected of the first murder, but police now have another man in
custody. Ironically, the suspect, Luke Surmanski, owner of Luke's
Lakeside Marina, was one of the co-sponsors of a hole in one prize
at the charity golf tournament.
The prize, a jet ski, was also sponsored by Arabella Carpenter and
Emily Garland of the Glass Dolphin antiques shop.
Readers will remember that Carpenter is Levon's EX-WIFE. This
blogger has discovered that Emily and Luke have been in a
relationship for some months.

The message Kerri was relating was clear: Luke, Levon, Arabella,
and Emily were in cahoots somehow, and had left Luke holding the bag.

"Kerri St. Amour at her finest?" Fran asked as she set down the
plate of French toast.

"She's all but accusing Levon, Arabella, and me of being
murder partners with Luke, who I am sure is not guilty."

Fran gave her a sympathetic smile. "I know you really like him,
hon, but the police must have some evidence to be holding him in
custody. Has he gotten bail yet?"

"I don't think so."

"I rest my...wait a second. Is that man in the photo Trent
Norland?"

"Yes, why?"

"Because that's my 'BLT double bacon, mustard, no mayo'
guy."

"Are you sure?"

"Positive."

Emily forgot all about being hungry and tired. She asked Fran to doggie bag the French toast minus the syrup, and poured some medium roast coffee into a to-go cup from the help-yourself bar while she waited. She needed to talk to Arabella. Now.

She power-walked to the Glass Dolphin, arriving to find Arabella happily sorting Heidi's quilts; a couple of quilts had already been hung up, looking more like works of art than something to put on a bed. Arabella looked up, surprised.

"It's tomorrow already?"

"No." Emily put her toast and coffee down, and handed Arabella the paper. Arabella skimmed through the content quickly.

"I was reading this at the Sunrise Café when Fran noticed the photo of Trent Norland. Turns out that he's the 'BLT double bacon, mustard, no mayo' guy. Which means——"

Arabella sat down. "Which means Trent Norland is…was… almost certainly Norrie."

"My thoughts exactly."

"We need to call Walker Lawrence."

The door chimed. Both women looked up. Elvis had entered the building.

48

WALKER PULLED a press back chair next to Emily and Arabella and sat down heavily. "Heidi Jacobs passed away last night. She went peacefully, with me by her side. I wanted to tell you both in person."

"Oh my god," Arabella said, fighting back tears. "I thought she had more time."

"That's what she led me to believe, too, but in reality, her cancer was far more advanced than she had let on. She made a new will last week. She bequeathed her house and property to Golden Rescue. Heidi had been fostering golden retrievers for them until she got sick. She was incredible with dogs, and they would often send her their most challenging rescues to get ready for adoption. The funny thing is, Heidi never owned a dog. She said she couldn't bear to have a dog die on her."

"What a wonderful legacy," Arabella said.

"There's more," Walker said. "She also left the bulk of her antiques to Arabella Carpenter and Emily Garland, co-owners of the Glass Dolphin, to be sold at their discretion."

Arabella couldn't believe it. They barely knew Heidi. She glanced at Emily and saw her surprise mirrored on her friend's face.

"She was very impressed with you and your store."

"But she'd never been in the store," Emily said.

"No, but a good friend of hers has been. He recently bought your marble clock."

"Windsor Scott?" Arabella asked, thinking of the number of times he'd been in, sometimes buying, sometimes just stopping by to chat.

"One and the same. Seems he told Heidi all about your store, long before she even met you. Once she did…well, remember, you reminded her of herself twenty years earlier? She didn't have children or family. To Heidi, you turning up that morning at the antiques mall in Thornbury was an omen. When you treated her with such respect at her home, not trying to rip her off, intent on being fair on the pricing, she knew her instincts were right."

"I don't know what to say," Arabella said. "Me either," Emily said.

"There's nothing to say. You'll have to wait until probate clears, of course, but you're certainly welcome to go to the house and do a complete inventory. There are a handful of items that will go to others on the list, myself included, although I plan to gift you the items she left to me."

Arabella frowned. "Why would you do that?"

Walker tried to smile, and didn't quite succeed. "That's the other reason I'm here. It's about Trent Norland."

"If you're here to tell us Trent Norland was Norrie, the man you started FYSST with, we've already figured it out." Arabella told Walker about Fran recognizing his photo as the BLT guy. "I'm sure Betsy at The Hanged Man's Noose will confirm it, as well. What we don't understand is why you didn't tell us. You had to know he was there the day that Marc Larroquette was shot. Why keep that from us?"

"I suspected that Trent had shot Marc, but I didn't have any proof." Walker shook his head. "Trent was a very troubled individual. I thought FYSST could save him. I was wrong."

"What did Marc do to Trent?" Emily asked.

"Marc was a blackmailer, as I'm sure you've found out. He may have stopped gambling, but he wasn't above making a living on the backs of other people's secrets, even when it came to his own stepdaughter, Chloe. He also knew something about Luke Surmanski's past—enough of a something that Luke agreed to rent a houseboat to him without proper identification. Using a boyfriend's name— a boyfriend that happened to be Emily's ex— was him being a sick bastard."

"You knew about all of that and didn't say anything when we were in Thornbury?" Arabella asked.

"Like I said. I had no proof, and I'm guessing about Luke. Then a week ago Trent came to me, looking for advice. He told me that he and Gilly Germaine were planning to rip off the Kids Come First charity. The golf tournament was a sham."

"A sham?" Arabella thought about the silent auction items so carefully selected by their donors.

How could Gilly have considered doing such a thing?

"Certainly some money would have found its way to the charity's coffers, but by no means all of it. Marc found out about their plans—I have no idea how, but he was one very resourceful blackmailer. Trent begged me to help him."

Walker managed a bitter laugh. "As if I was going to help bail him out yet again. I told him to go to the police with Gilly. Technically, they hadn't yet committed a crime. Trent said he had a better solution."

"And you think that solution was killing Marc?" Arabella asked.

"Imagine this scenario. Marc tells Trent he'll meet him at the third hole before the tournament starts. No one is going to suspect Trent of anything. As the hole in one insurance guy—a job he managed to secure with Gilly's help just days before the tournament —being there early was the responsible thing to do. Marc asks for a piece of the action. Trent says no. The two argue, and Trent shoots him."

"We're pretty sure Gilly stole Levon's gun," Arabella said. "She had a key to his house, and from what we can gather, Levon had either told her the combination or had it written down somewhere. Are you saying she took the gun and gave it to Trent?"

Walker nodded. "Levon had told her the gun was worth at least a thousand dollars, and maybe more. He was even naïve enough to tell her that it came with the original ammunition."

"Levon told me that isn't as unusual as you might think," Arabella said, not sure if she was helping or hindering Levon's case. "Ammunition can be sourced a number of different ways, it is easily made, and many antique shooters make their own ammunition."

"Levon taught you well," Walker said with a smile. "In addition, the original chambering of .476 caliber allowed a number of different calibers to be used. Some of those can still be purchased as specialty ammunition manufacturers are still producing them...I've owned a couple of antique firearms in my time, as well.

"But back to your original question. Gilly made the mistake of telling Trent, and he dreamed up a plan to buy Marc's silence for the gun. He claims that he had brought the gun to the meeting, not to shoot Marc, but as payment for Marc to stay quiet. The problem was Marc recognized the antique gun as Levon's. Instead of accepting it as payment, he challenged them. Was the gun theirs, purchased from Levon, or was it stolen? The two scuffled, and the gun went off."

"So it wasn't pre-meditated," Arabella said. "He could have told the police everything."

"Could have, sure, but Trent figured Levon would get the blame, given his past relationship with his father. Nice guy that Trent was, he had no problem letting Levon take the fall for it. Trent wiped the gun down to remove his fingerprints, and then hid the gun inside the jet ski. It was a risk, but a calculated one. He knew he'd be able to go back to the jet ski once the police cleared the scene, and he gambled that the police wouldn't find it. But even if they'd found the gun, he figured either Luke or Levon would be the ones suspected. Luke because it was his jet ski or Levon because it was his father."

"That's quite a story," Arabella said "I assure you it's true."

"Do you think Gilly knew or suspected Trent of the murder?"

"Without question. According to Trent, Gilly planned to put the gun back in the safe, but when Levon became a prime suspect, she worried that the police might start watching Levon's house."

"So we know how Trent came into possession of the gun, and why he shot Marc," Emily said, recapping. "What we don't know is who shot Trent or how the gun ended up in the pond."

"Actually," Walker said, "that's the easy part of this puzzle."

49

WALKER GATHERED HIS THOUGHTS. "Trent knew Heidi wasn't well and called her, offering to provide a professional appraisal of her antiques with the view of purchasing some, and she called me. Heidi never liked Trent, because she saw what he'd put me through these past few years. She assumed that Trent would get a honest appraisal, and then lowball her on everything."

"Surely he wouldn't stoop so low as to cheat a dying woman?" Arabella said.

"I wish you were right, but I'm quite certain that was the plan, not that Trent told me in so many words. I do know it was the reason he called Levon for a meeting. He'd seen Levon's silent auction donation for a household or estate appraisal, and Gilly vouched for Levon's expertise."

"Was Gilly going to be in on that scam, too?" Emily asked.

"I think it's likely. She may have cared for Levon on some level, but it didn't stop her from stealing his gun, and she had no qualms about cheating a children's charity. I'm afraid Gilly is all polish on the outside, and all tarnish on the inside."

"And Levon—" Arabella couldn't bring herself to finish the sentence.

Walker shook his head. "If it's any consolation, Levon had no idea about any of it. He went to that meeting with Trent unsure of what to expect. Thanks to me, he never had to find out."

"Why thanks to you?" Arabella asked.

"Because I phoned Trent and asked him to meet me on the trail behind the third hole. From this point on, I'm going to ask that you let me tell the story without interruption. Otherwise, I'm not sure I can go through with it."

"You have my promise," Arabella said. "Mine, too," Emily said.

Walker nodded, then resumed his narrative.

"I told him that I'd found a way to dispose of the gun. A spot where the police would find it, somewhere they wouldn't have thought to look before, but where it would firmly cast the blame on Levon. Trent hesitated, at first, and for a minute I thought he might have grown a conscience. Then he admitted that he was waiting for Levon at the clubhouse. 'Even better,' I said. 'When the police found the gun, people would remember Levon being there, waiting.' Trent arrived less than five minutes later. He must have run there to meet me. There was no preamble, no second-guessing about what was going to happen to an innocent man. He simply reached into the small of his back, pulled out the gun, and handed it to me."

Walker's voice broke. "The gun was loaded. I had a thought, 'why is Trent carrying a loaded gun?' And then I shot him. I had to, you see. I would have done anything to protect Heidi. Anything."

Walker put his head in his hands and began to cry.

50

ARABELLA, Emily, Luke, Levon, and Hudson sat around a table at The Hanged Man's Noose. It felt odd, to Arabella, to sit with Hudson and Levon at the same table, but both Levon and Luke had insisted that Hudson should be part of their celebration.

Luke and Levon had been cleared of any and all wrongdoing. Walker, however, had been charged with first-degree murder and that put a damper on the gathering.

Arabella had been surprised when Hudson had accepted the invitation to join them, although not ungrateful. She wasn't sure if the two of them had a future, but she did know she couldn't revisit a romantic relationship with Levon. Gilly and the key had cemented that decision and no amount of cognac would weaken her resolve. Not this time. Not again. Never again.

"So let's get this straight," Betsy said, after serving each of them a complimentary Treasontini. "The Kids Come First Charity Golf Tournament was a scam from the beginning?"

Arabella nodded and said, "Trent's doing, and possibly to a lesser extent, Gilly's."

"And Trent killed Marc because they thought he was going to expose them?"

Arabella frowned, "That's what they thought. Remember Gilly Germaine's fancy story about using a real gun, not a starter's pistol, to start the tournament? Levon showed her his antique Enfield revolver, which he kept in his safe. She stole it. The gun was supposed to be payment to Marc Larroquette so that he wouldn't report the scam, except when Marc saw the gun, he recognized that it belonged to Levon. The two struggled and it went off, killing Marc. It was an accident, but Trent didn't think the police would see it that way."

"The irony is, my father would never have gone to the police to report the scam," Levon said. "He spent his life avoiding them."

"What will happen to Gilly?"

"She hired Isla Kempenfelt to represent her on the charges of 'stealing a firearm and careless use or storage of a firearm.' Didn't you read the paper this morning? Kerri St. Amour says Gilly has agreed to take a plea deal of three to six months."

"But why did Walker shoot Trent?" Betsy asked.

"His animosity toward Trent has been building for years," Emily said. "They started FYSST and that meant a lot to Walker. Trent was willing to toss it aside if he smelled money. When Trent found out Heidi was dying, he tried to convince her to have an appraisal of her antiques with a plan to lowball the appraisal. That's why Trent was meeting Levon that day."

"He saw my silent auction donation at the golf tournament," Levon said. "An antiques appraisal for an estate. He wanted to hire me."

Arabella said, "Heidi told Walker that Trent had approached her about the appraisal. She was suspicious, because she didn't trust him. In her new will, there's a clause in it that expressly states Trent Norland is not to profit in any way from any appraisal or sale of her collection.

"When Walker found out why Trent was meeting Levon, he called Trent and asked to meet him on the trail behind the third hole of the golf course. He told him to bring the gun, that he would dispose of it. When Trent gave him the gun, Walker shot him. He threw the gun in the pond, sure that the police wouldn't blame

Levon. He'd wrongly assumed that Levon had reported the gun missing before the first murder."

"He was right about that," Luke said. "They didn't suspect Levon. They suspected me."

"What did Marc Larroquette have on you?" Emily asked.

Luke flushed and glanced at Levon, who nodded. "Levon and I shared a summer together at Camp Miakoda a few years back, although we didn't hang in the same circles. I didn't want anyone to know I'd been a young offender."

"It was a long time ago," Levon said. "We were kids on the wrong path. We're both different people now."

"What did you do?" Emily asked, her voice quiet.

Luke looked at Emily with such love that Arabella felt a moment of envy.

"I stole an expensive boat and took it for a joy ride, which I crashed into a private dock. It wasn't the first time, but because I wasn't eighteen I was tried as a young offender and sent to Camp Miakoda. My guess is Marc, being a blackmailer, had done his research on all of Levon's boot camp mates. He threatened to go to Kerri St. Amour. I knew how much Kerri hated Emily. I could just imagine what Kerri would do with the story. It wasn't so much about protecting me and the reputation of my marina, though that was certainly part of it. I wanted to spare Emily any further humiliation at the hands of that woman."

Emily put her hand in Luke's and squeezed it. "We all have things in our past we'd rather not talk about," she said.

"That we do," Hudson said. "Like the reason kids used to call me Banana."

"Banana?" Arabella asked. "Why Banana?"

"A story for another day." Hudson raised his Treasontini in a toast. "To old friends and new beginnings."

"To new beginnings," Betsy said.

"And to no more murders," Emily said. "I'm officially retiring my detective uniform."

"I'm going to hold you to that," Arabella said, clinking glasses with everyone. Was it just her imagination, or did Levon let his glass linger on hers a moment longer than necessary? She caught the look in his indigo eyes, and knew that the lingering touch had been intentional. She shook her head, ever so slightly, and put her hand in Hudson's. It was time for a new beginning.

Wasn't it?

ACKNOWLEDGMENTS

The idea for *A Hole In One* first came to me while I was golfing. As a longtime ladies league member of the Silver Lakes Golf & Conference Centre in Holland Landing, Ontario (the inspiration for Lount's Landing), it seemed only fitting to design the third hole of the Miakoda Falls Golf & Country Club based on the third hole at Silver Lakes (though there are no dead bodies in their woods). Beyond my often-too-vivid imagination, there are many real people who helped to make this book possible, especially:

Sarah Byrne, who bid on my "name a character" silent auction item at Bouchercon 2015 in Raleigh, North Carolina. Constable Sarah Byrne was born because of your generous donation to charity.

Kathleen Costa, beta reader extraordinaire, for her willingness to critique and correct with honesty and compassion.

Helen Farnsworth, a longtime member of the International Perfume Bottle Association, for her information on the Herman Tappan Perfume Company, as well as her suggestion for the Glass Dolphin's silent auction donation.

Anita Lock and Ti Locke, for their tireless editing efforts to make this book the best it could be.

Sean McGuire, www.oldguns.ca, for the suggestion to use an Enfield Mark I as the murder weapon, and for explaining why it was a good fit for the story.

Larry Owen, a good friend and former attorney, for his advice and guidance on legal procedures in Ontario.

Constable Andy Pattenden, York Regional Police, for answering my questions about antique guns and gun laws in Ontario (and for not sending an officer to my house).

Last, but not least, with love and thanks to Mike Sheluk, my husband, beta reader, and best friend.

ABOUT THE AUTHOR

Judy Penz Sheluk is the author of the Glass Dolphin Mystery and the Marketville Mystery series. Her short stories appear in several collections, including *The Best Laid Plans: 21 Stories of Mystery & Suspense*, which she also edited.

In addition to writing mysteries, she spent many years working as a freelance writer and editor; her articles have appeared in dozens of U.S. and Canadian consumer and trade publications.

Judy is a member of Sisters in Crime National, Toronto, and Guppy Chapters, International Thriller Writers, the Short Mystery Fiction Society, South Simcoe Arts Council, and Crime Writers of Canada, where she serves on the Board of Directors.

Find Judy at www.judypenzsheluk.com.

Made in the USA
Las Vegas, NV
11 March 2022

45438271R00125